I0736963

Praise for The Weird Girls Series

"Jam packed with action, suspense, kickass girls, hot guys, humor and all out weird girls, this series has me coming back for more and more." - **Night Owl Reviews (Top Pick)**

"I definitely recommend this series for lovers of all things paranormal and awesome."- *USA Today*, **HEA**

"Boasting an edgy, witty and modern style of storytelling, the reader will be drawn deep into this quirky paranormal world located in Tahoe, Calif. Strong pacing, constant action and distinctive, appealing characters - including a gutsy heroine – will no doubt keep you invested."- **RT Book Reviews**

"I would devour anything that Ms. Robson writes. I strongly recommend this series to PNR/UF readers and fans of Larissa Ione, Kresley Cole and Gena Showalter. Cecy Robson is pretty up there, IMO." *- Under the Covers Book Blog*

"Robson has once again created a master piece filled with longing, suspense, action, romance, danger, humor, friendship, family bond (in all forms) and kick butt heroines and heros that will work their way into your heart and mind and refuse to leave and that will be okay because you won't want them too."- **My Guilty Obsession**

"Okay, its official! Cecy Robson is one of the grand dames of cliffhanger finishes and she does it with like two sentences. She layers a shock on top of a shock so that I just sit there staring at the last page with a whimpering 'no, it can't end there' on my lips before hoping like mad that the next book is coming out some time this year or praying for strength if the release date is more than a year off...Urban Fantasy fans get busy and grab this series up. Paranormal Romance fans, you won't be disappointed either." - **Delighted Reader**

"Cecy Robson has been added to my favorite authors list and The Weird Girls series is one of my favorite urban fantasy series. Fans of Kim Harrison's the Hollows series and Patricia Brigg's Mercy Thompson series will devour Weird Girls."- **Caffeinated Book Reviewer**

"This series really does have it all, and in an increasingly crowded genre, it's a standout."- **My Bookish Ways**

"This series has everything paranormal romance and urban fantasy lovers could possibly want. From Action, to danger, to steamy hot romances, to strong characters and bonds, plus a bit of mystery and politics, what's not to love? I'm only sorry it took me this long to find this series...But now all I want is more and will be anxiously waiting until I can get my next Weird Girls fix." - **A Book Obsession**

"If you're a fan of urban fantasy or paranormal romance and you're NOT already reading this series... START!... From start to finish, Ms. Robson's writing is crystal clear and concise yet beautifully descriptive and YES, she can write the romance parts AND the fight scenes equally well. Hence why I have no reservations about recommending this series to just about everyone I know."
- **My Para Hangover**

"Cecy Robson is a phenomenal talent who knows just how to deliver a story filled with suspense, action, humor and romance…leaving you craving for more!"
- Romancing the Dark Side

"This book doesn't disappoint with its thrilling action, dangerous demons, spicy romance and original paranormal beings. I am a solid fan of this series as I love the originality, humor and adventure...If you are in desperate need of a recharging read, you must get these books!" -
Rainy Day Ramblings

"Cecy Robson is one of my absolute favorite authors and each book that she writes becomes more gut-wrenching and brilliant than the last...I'm dying to read the next installment."
- Books-n-Kisses

"Robson manages to take us into her world after a few pages and it is always very difficult to come out. Vampires, demons, werewolves and our dear sisters mingle to make an explosive mixture...If you have not tried this series, I highly recommend it to you. You will be blown away by the first pages and you'll be able to discover a world full of creatures of all kinds."
- Between Dreams & Realty

BY CECY ROBSON

The Weird Girls Series
Gone Hunting
A Curse Awakened: A Novella
The Weird Girls: A Novella
Sealed with a Curse
A Cursed Embrace
Of Flame and Promise
A Cursed Moon: A Novella
Cursed by Destiny
A Cursed Bloodline
A Curse Unbroken
Of Flame and Light
Of Flame and Fate
Of Flame and Fury (coming soon)

The Shattered Past Series

Once Perfect
Once Loved
Once Pure

The O'Brien Family Novels
Once Kissed
Let Me
Crave Me
Feel Me
Save Me

The Carolina Beach Novels
Inseverable
Eternal
Infinite

APPS
Find Cecy on *Hooked – Chat stories APP* writing as
Rosalina San Tiago
Coming soon: *Crazy Maple's Chapters: Interactive Stories
APP:* The Shattered Past and Weird Girls Series

A WEIRD GIRLS NOVEL

CECY ROBSON

Gone Hunting is purely a work of fiction. Names, places, and occurrences are either products of the author's imagination or used fictitiously. Any resemblance to actual events, locations, or persons, living or deceased, is entirely coincidental.

Copyright © Cecy Robson, 2018
Cover design © Kristin Clifton, Sweet Bird Designs
Formatting by BippityBoppityBook.com

Excerpt from *Sealed with a Curse* by Cecy Robson, copyright © 2012 by Cecy Robson
This book contains an excerpt from *Sealed with a Curse* by Cecy Robson, the first full length novel in The Weird Girls Urban Fantasy Romance series by Cecy Robson.

All rights reserved.

Published in the United States by Cecy Robson, L.L.C.

Print: 978-1-947330-11-5

Dear Reader,

The night I was born, a bat swept down in front of my father as he ran along a cobblestone road. My father ignored the bat in his haste to reach the Central American hospital where my mother labored with me. The bat disappeared into the shadows. In its place emerged a man, his dark skin bare, his voice ominous, his imposing form blocking my father's path. "Be wary of this one," he warned in Spanish.

"She's not like the others."

Okay, I'll confess. This didn't happen. But it sounds way cooler than simply admitting my father used to kiss me goodnight wearing vampire fangs and that he was the first person to trigger my overactive imagination.

I've always loved telling stories and getting a laugh. I've also enjoyed hearing stories, especially of the paranormal variety. Being of Latin descent, I heard many tales of spirits who haunt the night, of death lurking in the darkness waiting to claim her victims, and of circumstances that could only be explained by magic and creatures not of this earth.

The stories frightened me. I often slept clutching a crucifix, while my plastic glow-in-the-dark Virgin Mary stood guard on my nightstand. And, still, I begged for more.

Sometimes the beasties of the night bumped too hard and I swear I could see ghosts floating above me. I trekked on, despite my fear, surviving each night with my plastic protector looking on.

On May 1, 2009, I decided to write a story about four unique women, who must trek through their own darkness where super-nasties bump hard and bite harder. *The Weird Girls* series is the journey of Celia, Taran, Shayna, and Emme Wird, sisters who obtained their powers as a result of a backfired curse placed upon their Latina mother for marrying outside her race. Their story begins when the supernatural community of Lake Tahoe becomes aware of who they are and what they can do.

"Weird" isn't welcomed among humans, nor is it embraced by those who hunt with fangs and claws, who cast magic in lethal blows, and who feast on others to survive. I wanted to show that "weird" could be strong, brave, funny, and beautiful.

My "weird" girls will often face great terror, just like my seven-year-old frightened self, except without a glow-in-the-dark icon to keep them safe. Despite their fears, they fight like their lives depend on it, with only each other to rely on.

Sometimes, the darkness will devour the sisters. And, sometimes, good won't succeed in kicking evil's ass. But just like glow-light Mary, there is hope. And there is humor—often twisted, a little inappropriate, and always hilarious—very much like a father saying goodnight to his children wearing a rubber ghoul mask and owning a collection of fake fangs no adult male should possess.

Read on and check out my *Weird Girls* series. Maybe you'll find I'm really "not like the others".

~ Cecy

DEDICATION

To Aric and Celia.

Chapter One

Her name was Celia. I never saw her coming. I didn't know I'd needed her. But isn't that how love is supposed to work?

I hop downstairs. I don't mean I take the steps one or even three at a time. I mean I hop over the railing and leap from the second floor to the first, landing almost silently in a crouch, the backpack on my shoulders barely brushing against my spine.

I'm a *were*. A wolf to be exact. I can get away with leaping from landings physically, but not so much with my mother.

"Aric," she calls, turning away from the stove. "You're a *were*, not an animal. Take the stairs."

Dad looks up from reading his paper and smirks. "Listen to your mother, son."

I return his smirk and walk toward the kitchen. "Yes, sir. Sorry, Mom."

All eight burners are going on the stove. The smell of several pounds of bacon and more pounds of eggs stirred my senses when Mom first opened the fridge. Yeah, I'm *that* sensitive to smell, sight, sound, taste, and touch. And at fifteen, I'm *always* hungry.

I plop down next to my dad, allowing the pack to fall to my side. "Smells good," I say.

Dad sighs and turns the page. "It always does when your mother's in there. Not so much when we cook."

"Nope. We suck," I agree.

Mom's laugh draws my smile. My parents are supposed to lay into me and drive me crazy, force me to rebel, and scream at me when I do things they think I shouldn't. Except, jumping down a flight of stairs and leaving my mostly destroyed clothes on the floor aside, I'm a pretty decent kid with awesome parents.

I reach for the pitcher of freshly squeezed orange juice, yawning a lot louder than I intend. "Sorry," I say, yawning a second time when I fill my glass.

My knife slices into the butter the second Mom drops several pancakes on my plate. I'm ready to dig in when the scent of fresh buttercream finds my nose. Instead, I blink several times, trying to brush off my fatigue.

I didn't sleep much last night. My head spun with weird dreams that didn't make sense. I was wrenched backward and away from her. No . . . that's not right. *She* was ripped from *me*. They were taking her away from me. Whoever *she* was. I frown, remembering how bad it tore me up. I tried to hold on, tried to see her face. All I could make out were her delicate hands in mine. She sobbed, afraid to let go, while my eyes burned with rage-filled tears.

I was pissed and sad and . . . *broken*, except nothing I felt made sense. I didn't recognize her and I couldn't fathom why she meant so much to me.

The only thing I'm sure of is that a part of me left with her. And the way I feel this morning, it's still missing.

"Are you all right, son?" Dad asks.

I don't realize how hard I'm gripping my knife until I open my palm and all that's left is a warped piece of metal. My anger at losing her lingers and I took it out on the stupid knife.

"Sorry. I was . . ." I was what? Angry that I let some girl I didn't know go? "I didn't sleep well," I admit.

Dad folds his paper and places it aside, closely analyzing me. "Did you sleep with the window open?"

I don't remember leaving it open, but I nod when I remember how the cool spring breeze swept against my back when I stumbled into the bathroom this morning.

"There was a bad windstorm last night," Dad says, his dark eyebrows furrowing. "Earth's energy travels in the wind, as well as the memories of those long forgotten."

"The wind also carries magic," Mom quietly adds. She leaves the stove, a large pan of eggs gripped in her hand.

"Yes," Dad agrees. "A great deal of magic."

Mom scoops eggs onto Dad's plate, forming a large pile. "In the future, when the wind is that rough, I'd like you to sleep with the window closed."

The scent of cheese, carefully diced onions, and minced garlic seeps into my nose in a mouth-watering sweep. I dig into my eggs the moment the first scoop lands on my plate.

"Why?" I ask, swallowing quickly.

"You're different, son," Dad reminds me.

My chewing slows. It's the same thing I've heard all my life. Yeah, some things come easy for me. I'm stronger than older and larger *weres*. I'm a better tracker and more agile than anyone around. But I don't feel different. I'm just me, I guess.

"I'm serious, Aric." Dad tells me. "You achieved your first *change* before you were two months old. We went to sleep with an infant between us and woke with a wolf pup. *Two months*. I still don't think you comprehend the significance."

Maybe I don't. The most powerful *weres* achieve their first *change* at six months of age following a full moon. The weakest, closer to a year. If you don't *change* in the first year, you're more human and that's how you'll stay. It's something *weres* who mate with humans deal with. Not pures like us.

My fork hovers over my plate as I give Dad's words some thought. I shove the large helping quickly into my mouth when I sense him noticing. No *were* had ever before achieved a *change* at younger than six months-old. It makes me uncomfortable to be perceived as omnipotent. I'm not. Cut my head off or shoot me up with gold bullets, I'm just as dead as the next *were*. People around here forget that. They look at me like I'll single-handedly save the world, or some other impossible stunt. They fall all over themselves, cozying up to me, filling me with compliments they can't possibly mean. The kissing up, the bowing, the *groveling*…I hate it.

"There's no telling how strong you'll become or what powers you may inherit because of it," Dad says.

"I had trouble sleeping," I mumble. "It's no big deal." I don't want anyone making a big fuss over me. It bothers me more when my parents do it. Aside from my small and close-knit circle of friends, they're the only ones who still see me as Aric, not the savior others have come to expect.

Mom scoops another large helping of eggs onto my plate. Tendrils of steam drift from the pan. "Perhaps. Perhaps not," she says. "But if you're this sensitive to what the wind carries, sleep with the window closed. I don't want to risk a mental attack, or worse, while you're at your most vulnerable."

I open my mouth to argue. It's not that I can't shut the stupid window or that I need it open. I suppose I just don't want to focus on how different I am. I'm already weird enough.

Mom jerks. I cringe. My parents sense my discomfort and move on. Not that I like what they're up to.

"Aidan, behave," Mom whispers.

"What? Can't a wolf show his mate a little affection?"

She slaps Dad's hand playfully off her backside.

I make a face. "I'm right here," I remind them. "Can't that wait until I'm gone?"

"Not at all," Dad replies.

He pulls Mom onto his lap. If she were human, Mom would have spilled the eggs across the wooden floor.

"Eat with me," Dad tells her. "You're doing too much."

Mom kisses his cheek and places the pan on the table, allowing Dad to feed her. It's a mate thing. A protective thing. I've been exposed to it a lot in my life. But it always strikes me as intimate and something I shouldn't watch. I leave the table, returning with a large serving tray topped with bacon. I frown when I find Mom's arms wrapped securely around Dad's neck. Her shoulder length, white hair brushes against his chest with how hard she clutches him.

"You're going hunting again, aren't you?" I ask.

Mom lowers her eyelids as if in pain. Dad smiles softly at her, stroking her hair until she opens her eyes. She doesn't return his smile. It bothers me to see her upset.

"What's going on?" I ask.

"There's a dark witch causing trouble in Lesotho," Dad replies, continuing his slow strokes over Mom's hair.

I reach for more bacon and eggs. "Where's that?" I ask.

"Africa," Mom replies. "It's a territory known for diamond smuggling and dark magic."

"Cue the witch," I guess. Not all witches are dark. Last summer, I met Bellissima, one of the strongest light witches of her kind, along with her daughter, Guinevere, or was it Genevieve? It was something like that. They were okay. But dark witches really suck and give *weres* plenty of problems to chase.

As Guardians of the Earth, it's our job to protect the unsuspecting human populace from things that hunt them. Those creatures that go bump in the night? *We* eat *them*.

I shove a forkful of eggs into my mouth and stab a few more pieces of bacon. "How'd you hear about the witch?" I ask.

"She's protecting the diamond smugglers in the area," Dad explains.

I feel my eyes darken and a growl build deep within me. "In exchange for what?"

Dad doesn't blink. "Sacrifices, mainly human women and children."

I look to Mom, not liking where this is headed. "The women are deeply oppressed throughout the region," she explains. "When you find women fraught with worries of violence and struggling to feed their families, they tend to be more pure of heart and intent, and therefore easier to victimize. The children . . ." Mom straightens, passing her fingertips along the gray peppering Dad's temple. "There's nothing more sacred than a child's soul."

"Which makes the blood sacrifices she seeks more valuable. The purer the soul, the more power each kill will grant her," I finish for her. They nod. "Can I go with you?"

"No," Mom answers at the same time Dad says, "Maybe."

I perk up, my inner wolf totally losing it. "I can go?"

Mom shoots Dad a reprimanding look. "Aric is almost of age, Eliza," Dad gently reminds her. "He's far surpassed seasoned *weres* in strength, ability, and cunning."

Mom leaves Dad's lap, taking the empty pan with her. "No," she says.

Dad and I exchange glances. I know better than to speak up. Mom walks to the large porcelain sink and dumps the pan, gripping the edge. "Our world isn't what it once was," she says. "It's changing in ways even the wisest among us never predicted, Aidan."

Dad gets up slowly, briefly pausing behind her before his hands encircle her waist. He kisses her shoulder. "The world is changing," he agrees. "But it's our duty to maintain it, so good continues to prevail."

"There are many *weres* across the globe now," she reminds him. "Unlike generations ago, when our kind struggled to breed and flourish." She looks up at Dad, her soft brown eyes pleading. "Request that another pack or Leader go in your place. I hate it when you hunt. I hate it when you leave me. Please, my love, don't take our son, too."

"All right," he tells her.

"Wait," I interrupt. "Don't I get a say?" I don't know who's more bummed, me or my wolf.

Dad turns around, keeping Mom against him. "I need you here to protect your mother," he says.

I raise my eyebrows at him. He grins and so does Mom. She's almost sixty and Dad is seventy-five. Although they tried, they didn't have me until late in life. That doesn't mean either couldn't wipe the floor with anyone who messed with them. And if I wasn't around, Mom would be the one hunting alongside Dad, just as they did for years before I came along.

"Aric," Dad says. "I'm not yet sure I'm going. There's already a local pack assigned to track and kill the witch." He looks at my mother. "But in the chance I go, I won't upset your mother further by taking you along."

"Nothing's going to happen to you," I insist. "And if I'm with you, nothing will happen to us."

I mean what I say. My dad is unstoppable. A king among *weres* and my hero.

Dad offers a lopsided smile. "Aric, your mother is worried enough."

"I know, but—"

"*Especially* with all those females knocking on our door, seeking your company," he interrupts.

I roll my eyes. The females I know are annoying at best, looking to get with me for all the wrong reasons. "I don't even like them."

Dad barks out a laugh. "Not yet. But you will, son. It's just a matter of time."

"I just hope it's not any time soon," Mom quietly adds. She's still upset.

I rise, recognizing they need time. "Where you off to?" Dad asks.

"Hunting," I reply, excited for our plans and that we finally get a few days off from school. "Liam swears he scented elk near Mount Elbert."

Dad leads Mom forward, his fingers threaded in hers. "Is it just you and Liam?" he asks.

"No. Gemini is coming and so is Koda."

Mom exchanges a worried glance with Dad. "How is Miakoda?" she asks.

I shrug. When it comes to Koda, I walk a fine line between betraying my friend and keeping things from my parents. For the most part, I'm allowed free rein. They trust me, and I want to keep things that way. So, I tell them just enough to stay true to my friend.

"Koda's all right. He mostly stays at Liam's. The other night, he was with Gem."

Dad's voice grows an edge. "Do I need to pay his father a visit?"

My gaze lowers to the floor to hide my growing resentment of Koda's father. Except, resentment, anger, *any* emotion carries a scent my folks will recognize as easily as they take their next breath. It's the reason *weres* are so good at sniffing out lies.

Koda's relationship with his dad isn't like mine. Where I'd take a spray of gold bullets to keep my parents safe, Koda would run the other way with tears of agony mixed with relief likely streaming down his face.

"Aric," Dad says, his tone more severe. "Is Koda's father hurting him or his mother?"

"No," I answer truthfully. But only because Koda hasn't been around to let him.

Dad is a pureblood and Leader, just like Mom and just like me. Dad is also our pack alpha, the one who oversees *weres* and their activity within his territory. As formidable as he is, he's often tasked with solving matters outside our region that other *weres* can't handle. But his responsibilities are first and foremost to his pack. The same pack Koda and his family belong to.

"Aric," Dad says, this time more gently. "I'm only trying to help Koda and keep him and his family safe."

"I know." I meet my father square in the eyes, something most *weres* wouldn't dare do. "I'll try to talk to him today and see where he's at."

Dad nods, but he doesn't appear any less concerned. I can't blame him. Not after everything Koda's been through.

"Tell Miakoda he always has a home with us," Mom says.

"I will. Thanks, Mom."

My wolf stiffens when I bend to hug her. We have company. I release her slowly and turn toward the front of the house, my excitement building when I hear the voices of my friends.

"They're here," I say. "Gotta go."

"Be careful," Mom says.

I grin. "I'm going hunting, Mom. What could happen?"

I glide down the steep incline on four paws, digging my claws into the thick forest bed to keep my balance. The weight of my three-hundred-pound wolf form leaves deep indentations in the soil. There wasn't just one elk. There was a massive herd. We separated them as a pack, targeting the eldest and weakest, as nature demands.

The one I'm chasing stumbles down the ravine, his immense body crashing into the river bank and sending waves of muddy water to drench my face. I shake off the thick drops blinding me and hurtle forward. I'm almost on him, my excitement of snapping his neck and bringing home a feast propelling me faster.

I bare my teeth at the scent of his fear. Despite his weariness, he's fighting the kill. I can respect him as my prey. That doesn't mean I'll let him go. My supernatural strength jets me faster, ghosting over the slippery rocks when the elk stumbles. He quickly recovers on wobbly limbs. It doesn't matter. I have him. My family will have a sweet meal tonight.

We round the bend as I leap toward his neck. My fangs barely graze his tough pelt before I crash into what feels like an invisible wall. The force flings me backward, slamming me into the river bed. I whirl up, wondering what happened, and *pissed* that it did.

The sound of beating hooves grows distant as the elk disappears. I ignore his escape and growl with murderous rage.

Something's here. Something different. Something magical.

My paws keep my footing over the uneven and rocky bank as I stalk forward. I poke at the air with my nose, trying to sense the wall or whatever it was that caused my fall.

My nose twitches, latching onto something . . . *weird*. It's not elk, not deer, not even rabbit.

I smell predator.

A challenging growl rumbles through my torso and down my legs, causing a ripple across the water. My eyes sweep my surroundings, up the incline where the woods are thickest and back down where small, gentle waves splash over the river rocks.

Where are you? I growl again.

I angle my body to the left and frown. Something like rot permeates from the forest. It reeks of dead prey and danger, but then it moves further away from me and the predator I seek.

My eyes round with surprise when I hone in on a different scent. In the breeze, cascading along the bank, the fragrance of water misting over roses overtakes the aroma of pine, rich soil, and thick beds of moss, ensnaring me in its beauty.

An excited chill runs down my spine, standing my fur on end. I shake my head, trying to clear a scent that has no business latched to another predator . . . especially one warning me to keep my distance.

My ears perk up and my eyes hone in on a thick mound of blackberry brambles a few feet away.

There you are . . .

I prowl forward, my steps quiet and purposeful and my jaws set to sink into bone.

This isn't a cougar. They run from us.

This is hungry.

Dangerous.

Weird.

My body quivers with growing excitement and my thunderous growls echo. I snap my jaws in challenge, letting my prey know I sense him.

It's time to flee or fight. The choice is his. I'm not going anywhere.

The brush shifts. Slowly, very slowly, my prey rises. My lips peel back, yet the next growl dissipates before it can fully form.

Instead of fur, wet, wavy brown hair with streaks of gold catch the faint sunlight, spilling over slender shoulders and flawless olive skin, while droplets of river water trickle around large green eyes and full pink lips.

I stop breathing.

She's young.

My age.

And she's naked.

Chapter Two

"*Don't move,*" she hisses. "I don't want to hurt you."

Her voice is husky and lower than I would expect from a young female. It hooks my wolf and draws me closer. I pant, my tongue lolling over my sharp fangs before I realize it. I suck it back in, hoping she didn't notice.

That familiar sweep of magic that comes with a *change* feathers down my spine, dissolving my wolf form and tucking him back within my soul. I rise slowly from a crouch, my focus never leaving her.

Her eyes widen to frisbees and . . . she dives into the bushes.

"*Oh, my God,*" she squeaks.

I frown. "What's wrong?"

"You're *naked*!"

"So are you," I point out, wondering what the problem is.

"I'm—put some clothes on!"

"What?" I ask, sure I misheard.

"I told you to put some clothes on."

I glance around and motion behind me like a dumbass. "My pack is up there."

"There're more of you? Naked more of yous?"

Wow. She's really hung up on this whole naked thing. "I brought my friends," I explain slowly. "They're like my own pack. But I meant my backpack. That's where my clothes are. Up there. Near them. Where we left them, I mean."

I don't normally sound this stupid. I also don't normally meet females in the bushes. The females I meet tend to flirt and want to touch me, not shrink away like this one. I lean closer when she crouches lower and tries to cover herself with leaves. "Is something wrong?"

"You're a werewolf," she says.

She's not really asking. But it's also like she's not sure. "Yeah," I say.

"I've heard of you," she says.

My body heats with embarrassment. Great, another groupie in the making. "This is our territory and where we're most known," I say, trying to downplay my family's epic heritage, even though it's far from the truth. Thanks to my early freakish *change,* my already famous family is now world-renowned.

"Your territory?" she asks.

"That's right," I say, shaking off what remains of my awkwardness.

"Where?"

"What do you mean?" I crouch deeper, trying to see her face. All I catch are glimpses of skin. "Why are you so muddy?"

She waits, as if debating what to say. "I spent the night here. I was hungry and trying to catch some fish. I, ah, wasn't very good at it."

That doesn't sound right. I caught my first fish when I was three and I wasn't even trying. Being a predator, one with such a strong sense of magic permeating from her skin, she should be able to fend for herself.

"What are you?" I ask.

Her voice grows quiet. If I were human, I'm not positive I'd hear her. "Just tell me where I am. Please."

"Um, sure." I turn back around, when I hear the familiar sound of paws striking the earth. My friends are closing in, maybe a few miles out at best. My brow furrows when I catch another nasty whiff of that festering stench I smelled earlier. But as I turn back to the timid female, the stench dissipates and so does everything else. All that's left is her.

"We're on Mount Elbert," I clarify. "About ten miles from the closest highway."

Her pause is so dramatic it seems to still the air around us. "Where's Mount Elbert?"

"Lake County," I offer, wondering why she sounds confused.

She releases a shaky breath. "And where exactly is Lake County?"

"Leadville," I reply. "Colorado."

The pace of her breathing increases. "I'm in Colorado?"

"Where else would you be?" I ask.

"New Jersey."

I bark out a laugh. "Why would you want to be in that garbage dump?"

She groans. "It's my home."

"Oh. Sorry." I push down the brambles, avoiding the thorns as best I can to better see her. All I catch are the body parts she clearly doesn't want me looking at. She scrambles to the left where the overgrowth is at its thickest.

"What are you doing?" she asks.

"Trying to see you," I say. It seems odd to have to explain myself this much, and even more strange for her to be so guarded.

"I think you've seen enough," she replies stiffly.

"Come on," I say, laughing. "This isn't the first time I've seen a naked female."

"I'll just bet, big boy," she snaps.

"What do you mean?" Whoa, she's pissed. "My kind and I *change* all the time in front of each other."

"Great. Of all the places I could have been zapped to, I get sent to a nudist colony in Colorado."

"This isn't a nudist colony." I swipe my mouth,

choking back another laugh. "And I mean *change* form, not change clothes."

"Huh? Oh. You mean transform."

"No. I mean *change*." I cock my head. "You don't know a lot about us, do you?"

"I know enough."

"Oh, yeah?" I grin. "Like what?"

Her large eyes blink back at me. "Like you're strong and lethal."

My smile vanishes. We kill those who threaten us and the world. But that's not what she wants to hear. She's scared. "I'm not going to hurt you," I promise.

Her gaze softens with relief. It's not a lot. Just enough for me to think she might believe me. I wait for her to say something, anything, rubbing my nose when the wind picks up and the stench from that festering animal whips past my nose. The smell is awful, but it doesn't stand a chance against this female's sweet aroma. When she doesn't speak, I realize I have to.

I try to keep my voice casual and unthreatening. "Wolves, all *weres* really, *change* form around each other all the time," I explain. "Our beasts tend to be two to three times our human size. When you tear through clothes like we do, it doesn't leave a lot of room for modesty."

"I guess that makes sense," she says, her voice strangely innocent for a predator. "For your kind, I mean. But please understand, it's not something I'm accustomed to."

I want her to keep talking. It doesn't take a genius to see she wants to remain silent. "You said you got zapped here," I remind her. I take another whiff of her scent, trying to zone in on her emotions and figure out what she's thinking. All it does is warm my body further, flushing my skin. I clear my throat. "What did you mean by that?"

"It means I don't belong," she says.

The scent of sadness permeates the air between us. She doesn't just mean she doesn't belong here. She doesn't feel like she fits anywhere.

My wolf whines. He doesn't like her sad and neither do I.

I try to smile. "I'm Aric. Aric Conner. But I guess you already know that."

She tilts her chin and blinks back at me. "Why would I know that?" she asks.

Heat creeps up my neck. "You said you've heard of me."

"No . . . I meant I've heard of werewolves. That they exist. I've scented them around in New Jersey and came across a few. They weren't exactly friendly."

"No kidding," I mutter.

"Excuse me?"

Her brow crinkles. Whoa. She's really cute. I drag my hand through my hair, giving myself a moment to gather the confidence I first had when I found her. "What I meant was, New Jersey kind of sucks."

"Mm. Does it?" she asks.

"I don't mean you suck. I just mean your state sucks."

If I had my socks near me, I'd ram them in my mouth.

"You have a problem with New Jersey, oh, naked boy crouching in a creek?" she fires back.

By now, I should be the one trying to hide. Instead, I laugh. Call it humiliation or call it something else. "Yes, and it's a river." I smirk. "You know what they say. The only thing good about being from New Jersey is being *from* New Jersey."

She returns my smirk. It looks way better on her. "For someone whose idea of a good time is streaking through the woods and scratching behind his ears, you're pretty judgmental," she teases.

I chuckle. "I also have mad tracking skills."

She laughs a little, though she seems surprised by the sound. "Is that so?"

I grin, meeting her gaze through the thick brush. "I found you, didn't I?"

It's there, I see it, a small smile lifting the corners of her lips and casting a shimmer across her irises. "I suppose you did, Aric."

My smile dissolves at the way she says my name, the

warmth my shyness initially spurred spreading through my chest. *What is she doing to me? Is it magic? That same magic that built that invisible wall I crashed into?*

"Is something wrong, Aric?"

There it is again. "No, I just . . ."

Her fingertips trail along her cheek, pushing the muddy strands away from her face. "You just what?"

"It's nothing." I cough into my shoulder. "I just like how you say my name."

"Oh," she replies.

The surprise in her tone is obvious. I can sense it and her shyness warming the air. I shouldn't like the way she says my name as much as I do. Except, here I am, waiting for her to say it again.

"You know my name," I remind her when she quiets. "But you haven't told me yours."

She lifts her chin, her gaze fastening on mine. "I'm Celia," she says. "Celia Wird."

Her words are careful, filled with uncertainty and a little fear. I don't want her to be afraid. Not of me. I grin, pushing my hand through a small opening in the thick brambles. I ignore the bite of the thorns. "It's nice to meet you, Celia."

Her hand slides across my palm. Like a wave of sunshine breaking through clouds, warmth pulses through my hand, blazing a path through my veins and straight into my chest.

It doesn't hurt.

It doesn't sting.

It's . . . *incredible*.

I jerk away as if burned, gaping at my palm and back at her. "What did you do to me?" I ask.

She trembles, her breath releasing in short gasps.

"Celia," I say, when she doesn't answer. "What did you just do to me?"

The sensation recedes, leaving me empty. Without thinking, I reach toward her again, seeking more.

"What are you?" I ask, my voice heavy and raspy.

She edges away, staring at my hand. I know she's scared. I open my mouth, hoping to reassure her. But then she whirls, shooting up the embankment so fast I barely trace the movement.

"Celia, *wait—*"

Shock cuts my voice off like the slice of a blade. Celia, the young vulnerable woman hiding in the brush, is gone. In her place, a golden tigress, its fur coated in mud, charges through the terrain and up the bank in a blur of speed and grace.

I jet after her. My bare feet crush the moist debris until I *change* and my thick claws scrape into the soil, flinging it behind me.

Chapter Three

I'm known for my speed, but Celia is *fast*.

She zigzags through the pines, letting the long heavy branches slap against my face. Flashes of black fur appear in my peripheral vision. Gemini is here with his twin wolf. Koda arrives too, the fur of his massive red wolf blazing like fire at midnight. Liam isn't far behind, I sense him more than I see him.

We break through the clearing, racing at full speed. I catch sight of Celia, just as I realize where we are.

The cliff. She's going off the ledge if she doesn't stop.

I howl and snap my jaws, warning her. All that does is increase her speed, and incite my friends to howl and snarl. The thrill of the hunt and the proximity to what they perceive as prey stimulates their voracious hunger. Their keen sights are set on Celia, but she's not theirs to have.

She's *mine*.

Dirt and debris pepper me as she digs her claws into the ground, trying to stop. She's going too fast, the weight of her tigress pushing her forward. I leap, *changing* into my human form and snagging her front paws when she slides, rump first, over the cliff. I wrench her to me, slipping an arm under her belly and around her head.

I dig in my heels and haul her back. The sensation—the one I felt when I touched her—envelops me in all the good ways possible. I start to relax until claws rake across my chest and tear through my skin.

"Ouch, Celia!"

I hook my arm tighter to pull her closer. "Don't be mean," I snarl. "I'm only trying to help."

Our closeness amplifies the warmth between us. I try to fight it, but that fight is brief. Like before, the feel of her consumes me.

My body welcomes Celia like an embrace after a long, weary day. It relaxes me, despite how my heartbeat races and her presence further rouses my beast.

I groan, clutching her closer. "It's okay," I whisper into her ear. "I won't hurt you. I swear it."

I have no business saying what I do. I don't know her and she just clawed my chest to pieces. My skin burns with the speed in which my wolf's magic heals me. As the skin knits closed, an itch develops I can't quite scratch.

"Werewolves, the ones *not* from New Jersey, protect innocents. That's you. So, predator or not, I'm obligated as a Leader of my kind to see to your safety."

My words are merely a trace of sound against her ear. Having her so close makes me feel peaceful and I think she reacts to me the same way. She falls limp in my arms. Not from exhaustion or injury. No, this is something else.

Her heartbeat matches the speed of mine, pounding against my chest. She whimpers and releases a shudder, not what I expect from a creature close to matching me in strength.

"Shhh," I murmur. "It's all right."

I rise to a standing position, pulling her carefully with me. She's small for a tigress, not fully grown, but long and formidable.

I forgot about my friends, until I see them wagging their tails ferociously. Everyone, that is, except Koda. His dark, stormy eyes glint with suspicion. He's not happy. Seeing how he's glaring at Celia, seconds from biting her, I'm not happy, either.

Liam is the first to *change*, leaping into the air and pumping his fists wildly. He tosses back his long blond hair as he lands. "Yeah! Aric bagged a tiger." He points to Gemini. "And you thought that elk you brought down was the kill of the day."

Gemini *changes*. He's tall like me, but relatively thin. His almond-shaped eyes narrow. Like Koda, he knows all is not what it seems. His twin black wolf paces restlessly back and forth, refusing to break his focus from Celia.

"She's not a tiger, Liam," Gem tells him.

Liam frowns. "Sure, she is. She's got stripes and everything."

Gemini pinches the bridge of his nose. It's something we do a lot around Liam. "That's not what I mean."

Koda *changes*. I'm told I have a few more inches to grow. But Koda is already taller and massive, compared to the rest of us. The black hair he's growing out brushes against his shoulders. "What is she, Aric?" he asks, his stance as deadly as his tone.

"A ti-ger," Liam says, like we're stupid.

"She's a girl," I say. I do a double-take when I notice Celia has one paw over her eyes. "She's just, you know, a little shy."

"A girl?" At my nod, Liam hunkers down, edging closer. "I don't know, Aric. I say we eat her." He straightens, holding up his hand. "Who's with me? I call dibs on a leg."

A guttural roar tears through Celia's throat. I hang tight when my friends snarl in response, barely keeping her against me.

"You're not going to eat her, touch her, or go anywhere near her," I snap. "She's a girl—a human—and she's under my protection."

My friends exchange sour glances. They don't like what I say, yet they recognize my pledge for what it is. As a Leader, they can't go after Celia without challenging me to a fight.

"You sure about that, Aric?" Koda asks, his deep

voice lowering and menace dripping from each vowel. "Humans can't *change* and she's coated with magic."

"And fur. Don't forget the fur," Liam says. "Koda's right." He makes a whirling motion with his finger. "*That* is *not* human."

"Her name is Celia," I say, growing defensive. "And, okay, maybe she's not entirely human, but neither are we."

"We're *weres*," Koda presses, his aggression growing more pronounced. "We know what we are, and what we're not. Can you say the same about this thing?"

That peace Celia's presence granted me abandons me in a rush. Ire digs through my tensing muscles, leaving me and my beast with the need to rip someone in two. "Call Celia a thing one more time and you and me are going to have problem," I snarl.

Koda's thick brows knit together and every muscle on his hulking body clenches. I've challenged him. Leader or not, he can answer it. And bigger or not, he's going down if he does.

Koda stalks around, ready to cast the first blow or the last, usually with good reason. Liam was the first friend he made and I was a close second. We've never come to blows. I hope today won't be a first. Friends, real ones, should never have to fight like this.

Instead of prowling forward, he holds back, crossing his arms over his chest.

Gemini steps forward, his twin wolf taking a seat beside Koda. Koda is a hothead. Gemini always keeps his cool, the reasonable one when the rest of us are losing our minds. I think he's taking my side. Until he speaks.

"I don't like this, Aric," Gemini says. He watches us closely, keeping his hands loose at his sides and his stance unthreatening, even as he says what he does. "What if she's a witch? Witches can assume forms with potions and cast spells to ensnare you with their magic."

I glance down at Celia. I'm not stupid, nor am I so blinded by her that I don't give thought to what Gemini says. For all I know, this is some kind of mojo meant to confuse me. These feelings I sense swirling through my head and how my body reacts when we touch shouldn't affect me the way they do. I only spoke to Celia a handful of seconds. But it's like my wolf snaps his jaws at my reasoning and in the direction of my friends. He wants us to protect Celia. Like me, he senses her honesty.

"She's not a witch," I reply. "I'm sure of it."

"What about a shapeshifter?" Koda suggests. "There's a lot we still don't know about them."

"Shapeshifters require decades of blood sacrifices to their deity in order to gain the power to assume any form," Gemini replies, saving me the trouble. "Celia is too young to have caused such damage." He rubs his jaw, eyeing her closely. My wolf and I don't like it. Gemini realizes it and drops his hand away, trying to appease me. "Besides, I don't feel that darkness that's supposed to accompany their kind."

"How would you know?" Liam asks. "It's not like you've ever met a shifter."

"They carry the power of hell within them," Gemini patiently explains. "You can't carry something that menacing without our wolves noticing."

The reminder gives the others something to chew on. Liam and Koda ease back. Gemini doesn't, keeping his position and staring at Celia as if taken by her.

It takes some effort, but I manage to keep from growling.

Liam picks up a small stone and tosses it a few yards away. "I don't know, man. I still think we should eat her."

Celia makes a chuffing sound.

Liam frowns. "What was that?"

Celia does it again. This time louder.

"Is she laughing at me?" Liam asks.

I smirk. "It beats her trying to rip your throat out, like you deserve." I lower her to the ground like I would a kitten, instead of the beast who made mincemeat out of my torso. "I'm going to let you go. Don't run, okay? You're safe here with us."

Celia's tail whips back and forth. She doesn't trust

me, but she needs to. I crouch down, meeting her eyes.

"Aric?" Gemini warns. "What are you doing? She'll take it as a challenge."

Ordinarily, he'd be right. To look another *were* in the eyes is the equivalent of a shove and a pass to draw blood. "Celia isn't *were*," I remind them. I extend my hand slowly and stroke her head. Her fur is softer and different than mine, more like bits of cotton stretched out into tiny threads.

I've seen pictures of humans wearing fur coats of exotic animals and thinking them fools. But I suppose wearing a coat like this is the closest they'll come to capturing the strength of the beast.

"Give us a chance," I tell her. "By the looks of it, you don't have many choices."

She eyes me carefully with each pass of my hand. Man. I'm practically offering my hand as her next meal. Still, there's a part of me that believes she won't hurt me. Call me oblivious, but someone who blushes as much is she does isn't going to maw first and ask questions later.

"What if we got you some clothes?" I ask. "Would that help?"

She cocks her head. "Hey, Gemini? Can you send your twin back for my pack? For our packs? I think Celia will be comfortable if we're all dressed."

Gemini looks to his wolf. "Go," he instructs. "Don't be long."

Liam kicks at the dirt when he sees Gemini's twin wolf take off in a sprint. "Do we have to get dressed?" Liam asks. "I have to air these parts out every now and then." He motions down his body. "You hear what I'm saying? Some things need to breathe."

Celia grimaces and turns away, staring out over the valley. "Liam, she's a guest," I say, trying not to laugh. "And from what I can tell, she's seen enough of your parts."

Liam grins. "Has she seen enough of yours?"

Heat flushes across my skin. I'm not embarrassed by my body. I'm embarrassed that Celia's embarrassed, if that makes sense. "Yes, Liam," I bite out.

Liam laughs, his blond hair flinging away from his face from the force he uses to throw back his head. "Aric's got a girlfriend," he sings, ignoring the dirty look I shoot his way.

"What?" he asks Koda when Koda tells him to shut it. "It could happen. Nothing says a *were* can't like a, ah, well, whatever she is."

"But there are expectations that purebloods keep their lineage clean and unmarred," Gemini says.

My chin jerks in his direction and I have to squash back a growl. It's not that he's making things up. But he doesn't have to rub Celia's face in it.

I open my mouth to argue, to tell him those rules aren't as stringent as they once were. Except then I realize I'm opening a can of worms that Celia isn't aware of . . . and that Gemini's full attention is on Celia, his deep fascination with her growing more pronounced. Maybe her tigress has caught his wolf's interest. Maybe I shouldn't care. She had the same effect on me.

It's what I tell myself. That doesn't stop me from narrowing my gaze and edging to her side.

I crouch beside her, wiping my mouth to hide my amusement when she does her best to keep her eyes on the valley and not on me.

"See that river down there?" I ask, pointing east. I pause when it occurs to me that maybe she doesn't possess the keen senses we do. If so, maybe she can't see the sliver of water cutting through the thick forest, or hear the gentle beat of whitewater soaking boulders as old as time. She nods. It gives me hope that maybe we're not so different. "It's three times as wide as the river where I found you and every bit as long. So long as you follow it, you won't get lost. It leads to the main highway and home."

Her eyes shimmer with hope and she starts to rise. "Not your home," I quickly add. "Mine. For you, we'll have to find a different way."

Celia's head droops. Just enough to demonstrate her disappointment, but not enough for my friends to catch a glimpse of her vulnerability. I stroke her back, although maybe I shouldn't.

If my friends were upset, I wouldn't demonstrate compassion like this. I'd listen. I'd offer my perspective. And if things were really bad, we'd hug like bros. Except Celia is a girl and, well, as much as Dad always told me females are our equals, he stressed I need to treat them differently. "Be gentle and respectful and mainly careful." I'm not sure this is what he had mind, but here I am.

My fingers glide between Celia's shoulder blades, over muscle lethal enough to kill, yet emanating enough warmth to soothe a treacherous beast like me. "I'll help you find your way back," I promise.

When her eyes meet mine, I swear I stop moving. The shimmer of green across her irises bespells me. It's not magic, not like Gemini claims. Nor is it evil disguised as kindness, like Koda inferred. It's just . . . Celia.

The thump of quick and agile feet approach. Gem's twin has returned and still I don't look away. Celia is the first to break eye contact, appearing startled by her reaction.

I drag my hand through my hair and mutter a curse. We're not exactly alone and we just met. The others are watching and judging and who knows what else. I'll deal with them later. Right now, it's about Celia and making her feel safe.

The wolf's heavy paws crunch the dried pine needles and bits of bark scattered along the plateau. Gemini's twin is usually ghostlike, blending into the environment as easily as our primal ancestors. My guess is that his loud steps are intended to not alarm Celia. He's cautious around her and he appears as fascinated by Celia as I am.

He lowers my pack at my feet, carefully backing away as if intruding on something intimate.

"Thank you," I tell him, kneeling and bowing my head so he doesn't notice my unease.

I position the pack so I can open it like a suitcase, wondering if I have anything Celia can actually use. The wolf edges away, his keen sight bouncing from me to Celia.

I jerk my head, trying get the wolf to give us more space. As much as he's a part of Gemini, he's more a twin to Gemini's wolf than twin to Gemini himself.

Gemini's mother was pregnant with twins. She didn't know, until she lost one and the Omega wolf who treated her told her she was still pregnant. They didn't expect the wolf spirit of the twin to survive. He did and joined the other who inhabits Gemini's soul. Like many strong *weres*, Gemini *changed* at six months. But instead of one wolf, he became two.

"Go," I mouth, when he sits just a few feet away. I'm doing my best to look cool in front of Celia, but the wolf is making it hard. He wags his tail, his full attention on Celia.

I unzip the pack and rustle through it. Aside from the jeans and black T-shirt I wore here, I have a pair of sweatpants shoved beneath my sneakers. The sweats will work fine. Celia can roll them and tie them or something. I shove my hand down to the bottom to retrieve the gray shirt I've likely had since our last excursion. I pause. Instead of offering Celia the gray shirt, the clean one, I hand her the black one I wore here, reasoning my scent will comfort her.

Maybe I shouldn't. It's like I'm marking her as mine, or something equally as crazy.

I clear my throat and offer her the sweatpants and shirt. "We can turn our backs if you want. Or, if it's better for you, get dressed behind those trees over there."

It takes a moment for Celia to lift the clothes from my grip, her powerful jaws careful as they clench the soft fabric. I start to say something more in the hopes to calm her fear about us, but the words lodge in my throat when I catch my friends' slacking jaws. Even the wolf is gaping at me.

"Problem?" I ask.

"Aric," Liam says. "What did you just do?"

I lie, since I don't know myself. "Nothing. Just turn around and cover your eyes or something. Celia needs to get dressed."

Liam crosses his arms. "I think it's only fair we see her as she is. She's seen us, right, boys?"

I know Liam is just curious about Celia. She isn't like anyone, or anything, we know. Still, I'm ready to pelt him in the head with a rock.

Koda storms away, giving us more space than we probably need. "You heard him, Liam. We're making Celia uncomfortable. You know better than to do that to a female."

It takes hearing those words for Liam to finally see the light. "Sorry, Celia. I didn't mean to make you feel that way."

Celia eases her way toward the trees. I'm not sure if I should follow. But then my beast doesn't give us a choice. It's like my wolf *needs* to be by her side and ensure she's safe. I allow him to guide me and lead us forward, his senses enlivening mine as we shadow Celia. He recognizes something within her that I haven't yet discovered. I want to, though. There's a reason she's here. I just have to figure it out.

"Can we at least watch her *change*?" Liam asks. He raises his hand. "I'm asking for strictly scientific purposes."

"What does that even mean?" I ask.

It's Gemini who answers. "He wants to see if she *changes* like we do or if it's different."

I shrug, trying to downplay my answer. "It's similar. Maybe a little faster."

Gemini raises his eyebrows. "Faster? We're pretty fast, Aric."

I recall how I only barely tracked her *change*. "I know," I say. "Just let her call the shots, okay? If she wants to show us, she'll do so when she's ready."

Celia turns and tilts her head. I can't guess what she thinks of me. I hope it's something good.

"Take your time," I say. I smirk when I realize she's working hard to keep her attention on my face and nowhere else. "We'll wait for you as long as it takes."

Celia's steps are hesitant as she walks past the wolves. She speeds up once she clears Koda. I'm certain she'll take off and I jog after her, trying to keep some distance yet not quite managing as much as I intend. My wolf is drawn to her tigress. Like an invisible rope, she pulls him along, encouraging him to keep close.

I force myself to stop when she reaches the edge of the forest and disappears behind an old oak, the trunk is massive. I suppose it suits her need for privacy and maybe gives her time alone.

I force myself to turn away, so she doesn't find me waiting for her like a lovesick puppy. I'm just in time to face Koda's reprimanding glare.

"Aric," he says. "What are you trying to do here?"

My stance tightens as I try to beat back the heat creeping up my neck. "Get her to trust us," I reply.

"Get her to trust *us* or score yourself some hero points?"

All right. I see where he's headed and I can't really blame him. Wasn't I the one who found females annoying just this morning? "I'm not sure what you mean," I reply. Hey, just 'cause he made the right call doesn't mean I have to own up to it like a wimp.

"Yes, you do," Gemini says. He's not mad, not in the way Koda is. But he is questioning my decisions, something that doesn't sit well with me as an alpha.

"Are you accusing me of doing something immoral or something that goes against our pack?" I question. "Or are you telling me I should have left her where I found her to fend for herself?"

Gemini lowers his chin, admitting defeat. "Yeah," I say slowly. "That's what I thought."

Liam's focus jumps between us, worry keeping him silent. He seems to want to say something, but just as he starts, he quickly shuts his mouth.

Celia steps away from the tree, pushing her long wavy hair back from her face as she steps carefully through the withering grass. The sweatpants are huge on her and she had to roll them many times so they'd stay on her tiny waist.

I may have more to grow, but Celia has reached her limit. She's small. But she must be tough to have survived the harsh forest elements overnight.

My lips press tight as I try not to laugh at how sweet

she looks. My T-shirt hangs low enough to be a dress on her and mud streaks her cheeks in rough and awkward lines. Aside from the few glimpses I caught when we first met, this is the longest I've looked at her human form. Like before, I can't get enough of her.

"Whoa," Liam says. "You're really pretty."

"Um—"

"I mean hot. Really hot." He nudges Koda. "Hey. Isn't she hot?"

"*Liam*," Koda spits out through his teeth. He motions to where I'm standing and not smiling anymore.

"Oh, sorry," Liam says. "I meant sexy. Is sexy a better word for you Aric?"

My mouth pops open. How has Liam survived this long?

Celia's hand covers her face. It doesn't quite hide her blush, nor keep her from turning into a shy kitten instead of a formidable tigress.

"Thank you for the clothes," she stammers. "If you could, I really need to find a way back to Jersey."

"Why?" Gemini asks. "Who's there?"

"My sisters and foster mother," Celia replies. Again, she's guarded, not wanting to give too much away.

"You have sisters?" Liam asks. "How many?"

Celia crosses her arms. "Three."

"Cool," Liam says. He inches closer to her. "Are they pretty like you?"

"We have similar features," Celia cautiously answers.

"They're golden tigers, like you?" Liam presses. He holds out his hands. "Wait. I know—

don't tell me. They take the forms of other big cats. A lion, maybe? How about a cheetah? I like cheetahs. Well, the ones I've seen on T.V., anyway."

Celia stiffens. Liam needs to back off, and I should tell him. Except, like the rest of us, he's curious and wants to know more.

"I'm the only one with an inner beast," she replies. "They . . . they're different."

"Different from you?" Liam asks.

"From everyone," Celia responds. Her demeanor turns grave. I don't quite understand it. It's like her sadness is too much to bear. "We're different from any race of human, *were*, or vampire on earth."

"Weird," Koda infers.

Celia's tiger eyes replace her own and hurt and anger flake off each word she speaks. "That's one way to describe us."

Koda glances away. "Sorry. I didn't mean to offend you."

I didn't like how Koda referred to Celia or how his comment affected her. I came close to storming over and making him apologize. Except, for all Koda is like a dangerous cloud waiting to storm, he's not cruel, especially when it comes to females.

Liam blows blond hair away from his face and grins. "You didn't answer my question, Celia. Are your sisters pretty, like you?"

Another splash of red against her cheeks is just what Celia needed to erase her anger. The truth I scent behind her words lift her lips into a small smile. "They're beautiful," she replies.

I return her smile, but it doesn't last.

Dread punches me in the gut and I whip around in the direction of the woods. That smell—that disgusting festering smell I caught earlier—saturates the air and coats it in a vile yellow mist, snuffing out the fresh breeze.

Gemini's twin wolf barks with pure rage and dashes into the woods. We growl as a pack, including Celia. There isn't a need for words. Something evil this way stalks and it's up to us to destroy it.

I prowl forward, my friends and Celia following closely.

Gemini's twin cries out in agony, the sound of splintering bone cutting off his tortured whimpers.

Gemini's eyes fly open. "*No!*" he yells.

"What's happening?" I snarl. "What do you see?"

Gemini's dark eyes gleam in that way they do when he sees through the eyes of his twin. "It has us," he rasps. He falls forward on all fours, clutching his neck. "It's coming."

"Screw this," Koda rumbles, taking off in sprint.

The twin wolf skyrockets from the thick stand of trees, landing at our feet with his head twisted at an odd angle. Gemini races to him, gathering him in his arms and hoisting his sagging body from the ground.

Koda stands a few feet from the dark forest, cemented in place, his attention on the spot where the yellow mist seeps out in thick tendrils. "What the hell is that?" he growls.

I grind my teeth. "Fall back."

Koda shakes his head stiffly. "No way."

"*It's not a request*," I bite out.

Koda backs up, the filthy yellow air that follows him morphing into a gelatinous, suffocating amber.

Celia and Liam gag, choking on the smell. I shove the bile burning its way up my throat, whispering low. "Liam, take point on the right, Koda, the left. Gemini, where's your twin?"

"Hidden, but unable to fight," Gemini says. "Something's wrong with him, Aric. He's not healing."

"If he can't heal, we may not be able to, either," I say. I don't mean to be blunt, but they need to know what we're up against and fight smart. Liam spits on the ground and Koda releases another few swears.

"Gemini, take the rear," I order, my hackles rising when I sense something drawing closer. "We'll see to your wolf when we're done tearing this thing apart. Stay sharp and keep Celia behind you."

"I'm no weakling," she insists. "I can help you fight it."

"This is our battle, not yours," I tell her.

Her resentment claws at my back. I don't bother arguing with her. We *change* into our beasts, ready to protect. Ready to fight. Ready to kill.

Liam's amber and brown fur blends into the mist, not that it will help us. Whatever approaches is manipulating this power in its favor. I rack my brain, trying to sort through all the entities I've studied to put a finger on what this thing is.

I don't wonder for long. Like a weary, old man, dragging his legs behind him, the mist parts and the creature emerges.

No. Not just any creature. A skinwalker. One of the few beings that are impossible to kill.

Chapter Four

There are legends of skinwalkers spoken in whispers. My
grandfather was one of the few *weres* brave enough to speak
of them after sundown. As Guardians of the Earth, we fight
dark entities who threaten our world. We're brave and strong,
but neither our prowess nor our beasts can shield us
completely from fear.

Skinwalkers are said to be *weres* damned to hell for
turning on our kind. My grandfather didn't agree. "No *were*
can commit such atrocities to deserve a fate like that,"
Grandad said.

"Then, what is a skinwalker?" I asked.

"A creature born of the evil man has committed upon our
earth. It cannot be killed. It doesn't bleed. It simply ravages
anything in its path." Next to Dad, my grandfather was the
toughest *were* I ever met, yet he shuddered as he explained.
"Dear boy, it's the one creature I pray you'll never meet."

I now understand why.

The first thing I see is the head of a festering stag, its
sixteen-point rack appearing too large for his willowy and
hunched frame. He stands on hind legs, the hooves stamping
into the soil like a being four times his weight, while long-
clawed hands drag grooves into the soil.

Chunks of rotting fur drop in wet clumps as he approaches. What flimsy hide remains, covers his shoulders and face in uneven and withered patches. His ribcage is fully exposed, revealing wads of shriveled intestines and mismatched portions of a liver and lungs.

There's no heart. He doesn't need one. Malice enshrouds him like a plague, alerting those in his path of their impending doom.

Anyone else who crossed him would be easy prey. Not me. Not my friends. *Not Celia.* My wolf releases an unearthly growl, converting my fear and shock to rage. I thunder forward, leaping into the air and using the full weight of my body to nail him like a battering ram.

My claws puncture through his ribcage and into what remains of his lungs, the bones cracking like splintering wood beneath my weight. I mistake this for an easy win, but the bones quickly reform around my paws, trapping me, and tightening around me when I try to wrench free.

His breath releases in a long exhale through his snout, delivering more of that vile mist directly into my face. I can't breathe, choking on air that punches its way down my throat.

Koda and Liam have his long talon arms pinned to the ground, and Gemini is trying to control his legs. The retching sounds they make obstruct their focus. But they can still breathe. I can't.

The mist coagulates into a gelatinous lump, blocking my windpipe. I attempt to warn my pack, but every movement expands and solidifies the lump.

I thrash. I won't give up . . . but neither will this skinwalker.

The skinwalker screeches like a thousand feral cats, shattering my left eardrum as he flings Koda away like a toy. Koda is close to four-hundred-pounds of muscle in his wolf form. He collides into the tree Celia dressed behind. The large trunk crumbles.

So does my friend.

I writhe, breaking my right paw free only for the decaying bones to reform and sink their shards into my flesh.

I use the weight of my hind legs, digging them into the skinwalker's pelvis and raking my rear claws through his guts.

I think I hurt him, but it's Gemini who pays. The skinwalker kicks his hooves into Gemini's chest, pulverizing his torso and sending him soaring backward.

Tears from the lack of air cause my vision to spin. I'm fighting half-blind, barely able to make out what's in front of me.

Liam's jaw crunches over the skinwalker's throat. I think we have him until Liam falls into a seizure, resuming his human form and foaming at the mouth.

"Don't bite him!" Celia yells when I snap my jaws. "His body is poison."

My vision fades in and out and Celia is suddenly there, clutching a large boulder in her hands. She brings it down on the skinwalker's head, cracking his snout and making him scream.

The skinwalker flails his clawed hands, trying to reach Celia. She ducks and jerks out of the way, lifting the boulder again and smashing it into the creature's face. The weight and force indent his snout, preventing it from reforming and releasing more rancid mist.

The lump in my throat loosens enough to allow a small wheeze. It's then Celia realizes I'm choking.

"*Aric.*"

This time when Celia slams down the boulder, the skinwalker's arms flop at his side. She leaves the heavy boulder in place and scrambles to me, her nails protruding into razor sharp points.

Celia grunts as she uses her claws to puncture the skinwalker's chest, cracking open the cavity so I can break free. I collapse on my side. My front paws are stripped of fur and my lungs are on fire. I know I should move, but right now, and I can barely focus.

Celia hurries to my side and rolls me over. I think she means to haul me away, but then her fist rams me in the gut.

I'm vaguely aware of her actions as I lose consciousness. It's only when I feel that lump of thickening waste dislodge in a painful jolt, that I realize what Celia was doing. I tilt to my side, spitting out blood and foam and whatever putrid waste the skinwalker fed me.

Like a row of daggers, Celia's nails elongate as she backs away. I'm breathing hard. I can't see much, but it's enough. The skinwalker shoves away the boulder and rises, that torturous screech blaring as he stalks after Celia.

"You want me?" she challenges. "Come get me."

The earth trembles beneath me as I push up to the side, each step the skinwalker takes toward Celia rattling the ground.

Earthquake, I think, pushing myself forward. *No. Not now*.

The ground splits in front of the skinwalker, the zigzagging crevice shooting toward Celia as if aimed. Still she taunts the skinwalker, keeping his attention while she leaps away from the dismantling ground.

"Come on," Celia snarls. "Is that all you've got?"

The skinwalker screeches, charging straight at Celia. He doesn't know I'm on my feet, ready to make mince-meat out of his hide.

The crevice breaks off in multiple points, creating a cobweb of deep fissures. Celia scrambles ahead and toward the cliff, leaping left and right, narrowly missing falling through the expanding cracks.

Her head whips around and she catches my eye. It's only for a second, long enough for her to realize she won't fight this thing alone.

Celia's final leap is the longest and most daring. She barely makes it onto the sole pillar of earth protruding from the ground. What remains of this part of the mountain has collapsed around us in a booming sound of noise and chaos.

The pillar is just a few feet in diameter. Celia barely keeps her balance, teetering back and forth as the ground trembles. The skinwalker jumps, his claws outstretched as he takes flight.

His strength is no match for Celia's. She knows it, yet she meets him dead on, her arms out and her nails ready to slash.

With all the strength of my hindquarters, I push off the ground, soaring into the skinwalker and throwing him off target. It's not hard, he's too far ahead. It's just enough to tilt him at an angle, making it easier for Celia to sever his spine.

The lower half of the skinwalker spirals into the gorge. The upper half snags Celia's waist, wrenching her down as the pillar tips at an angle. I slam against the side and slide after them, digging my claws through the soil to help me steer.

I catch up to Celia halfway down, her long nails stabbing the earth to keep herself in place as she kicks at the skinwalker holding tightly to her legs.

I lift my paws and increase my speed, ramming him hard. He barrels down the side, screeching, arms flailing with rage.

My speed and weight worked well to bring down the skinwalker, but now, they work against me. I barely manage to shift my weight and drive my claws into the ground to keep from joining him.

He disappears deep into the earth, the last of the sickening mist coursing behind him.

A screech of pain accompanies the first breath of fresh air filling my lungs. We did it. We brought him down.

My relief is brief. Slowly, the ground begins to reseal, the broken chunks of earth rising and filling the gorge. I glance up to see Celia looking down. Claws protrude from her toes, while the rest of her remains human.

Neat trick, but now is not the time to ask her about it. I climb up as fast as I can, encouraging her forward with a nudge of my nose. The ground is rising faster, loudly, like a crater being formed in reverse.

Celia grunts and groans each time her claws spike into the ridge. She keeps her head down, attempting to shield her face from the bits of dirt and gravel raining down on our heads. She's exhausted and weak from lack of food and water. Yet, here she is, moving as fast as her body will allow.

We barely make it out before the ground mends shut, falling on our sides and breathing hard. I turn, watching her claws dissolve back into her skin. She tilts her head, her dirt coated face meeting mine. "Just so you know, this sort of thing doesn't happen in Jersey."

Magic feathers along my spine as I *change* back, my lopsided smile widening when she covers her eyes. "Colorado's seen better days," I confess.

"Come on," I say rising. "We have to find my friends."

"First things first." She digs into the pocket of my sweats and pulls out a pair of boxers.

I chuckle and pull them on as fast as I can. I forgot I'd shoved them in there.

I stand over her when she continues to lie on the ground and offer her my hand. "Celia, I'm dressed. Now, come with me. The skinwalker has returned to its domain, but I can't be sure he'll stay."

Her eyes widen and she clasps my hand. I shudder when another wave of that gentle warmth surrounds us, struggling to focus on anything past her.

"My friends," I repeat. "We have to find them."

Celia releases me, staring at her palm, as if whatever connection we share will somehow be explained. "All right," she says, startling when a stand of trees pokes through from the ground. They twist up and out, spreading their long limbs and resuming their original form.

"Did the skinwalker do that?" she asks, following me as I head forward.

"No. It's the power of good within nature. The skinwalker was only about the evil that's been done to it."

My nose twitches when it picks up the scent of blood. *Koda's* blood.

I take off, back in the direction of the river. We find my friends further down from where I met Celia, hovering near an old fallen tree.

Gemini has resumed his human form, his pale body leaning against the bank and his twin wolf draped across his lap. He turns his head when he sees us approach. Koda kneels over Liam, whispering low. Like Gem, they're human and partially dressed, the sweatpants they wear muddy and torn.

Koda whips around, hanging tight to his stomach and snarling when he hears us approach.

He drops his hand away when sees us. "You're alive," he says.

Blood oozes from the wound in his stomach. If he's still mending, the injury was worse than I thought. "What happened to you?" I ask.

He glances behind me where Celia is standing. "It's nothing. I'm fine."

"What happened?" I ask again, this time louder.

"I was impaled. Like I said, I'm fine." He jerks his head to the side. "They're not."

My feet splash through the mud as I fall at Liam's side. His alabaster skin is saturated with sweat and his eyes stare blankly at the overcast sky. "Why didn't you *call* for help?" I ask.

"Our phones are dead," Gemini says. "We howled like crazy. No one came. Between the distance and the earthquake, I'm not sure anyone can hear us."

Gem's hand passes along his twin wolf's fur. The twin's neck remains at an angle and his deadpan eyes dart back and forth.

Celia kneels beside them. "Why are you so sick?" she asks Gemini.

Gem motions to his twin. "He's a part of me. I think we're dying."

"No," Celia insists. "You and Liam were poisoned when your wolves bit that creature." She looks around. "We have to get whatever you swallowed out. Can you throw up or something?"

Gemini shakes his head slowly, the effort appearing to rob him of his strength. His hand falls still over his twin. "It's deep in our stomach. I feel it expanding. I thought it was blood."

"No. It's poison, like Celia says," I agree. "We have to cut it out of you."

Koda scans his surroundings. "A stick. We can sharpen a stick."

"It won't be enough," I argue.

"Then I'll bite through it!"

"And swallow the same poison we want to get out?" I snap. "You're angry and scared, I get it. But we're on our own and we have to play it smart."

My attention falls on Celia, where she's petting the wolf's head. As her eyes assume that of her beast, I realize she already knows what I'm about to ask. That doesn't mean she's happy.

I kneel beside her. "We need something sharp," I remind her. "Celia, I need you to cut open my friends."

Chapter Five

Celia rises on wobbly legs that have nothing to do with hunger or weakness. She shakes her hands. "I need to wash my hands. They're dirty. I can't . . ."

The slow shake of my head causes her voice to trail. "Mud, dirt, bacteria—none of it will harm our system. But the skinwalker, whatever he left inside my friends, is killing them. You have to get it out." My attention falls on the wolf. "Gemini's twin goes first. He's been infected the longest."

"Can you tie his snout?" Celia asks. "He's weak, but I'm afraid if he startles, he'll try to bite me." She wrings her hands. "My tigress won't take kindly to anyone hurting us."

"You have nothing to fear," Gemini murmurs. "We would never hurt you."

The muscles along my spine pull against the bone. I shouldn't feel like this. Not now. I spit out a curse and refocus. "Koda and I will hold him just in case."

Koda fixates on Celia. "Aric, you sure we should do this?"

"The only thing I'm sure of is that we'll lose them by nightfall if we don't." I place my hand on his shoulder. "I trust Celia, Koda. I need you to trust her, too, so we can help our friends."

Koda hesitates only briefly. He understands what's at stake. "I'll take the top half. If he puts up a fight, I'll be the one he bites first. Aric, you get the legs."

"Belly up?" I ask.

"Yeah," Koda replies. "It will give Celia the best access."

Gemini slumps to the right when Koda and I lift the wolf from his lap, his eyes closing.

"You want something to bite down on?" I offer.

"No," Gemini slurs. "I need to guide you."

We lay the large wolf where the muddy bank flattens out. His breathing is nearly imperceptible. I listen hard, exchanging a firm glance with Koda.

The wolf's heart is barely beating. If he goes, Gemini will follow. "Celia," I call over my shoulder. "We need to move fast."

She rises from where she's bent over the river. "I'm coming."

Although we told her not to, she washed her claws. Water drips down the length of her blade-like fingertips, casting a sheen of silver in the dulling light. It's then I see how shredded and banged up her feet are.

"Why aren't you healing?" I ask when she settles between us.

Koda does a double-take when he sees Celia's mangled feet. "Did you swallow some of that crap, too?"

Celia stares at the belly of Gemini's twin. "No. I heal at a human's pace."

"You took on the skinwalker and you can't heal?" I don't mean to yell, but that's exactly what I do.

Her gaze melts into mine. "I couldn't just leave you." She averts her chin when she catches herself. "Let's get started. We're wasting time. Gemini, where do you want me to cut?"

Gemini gasps. "Start from the sternum and go down in a straight line toward the groin." It's taking all he has to remain conscious. "Hurry. It's trying to tear into my small intestine."

I speak fast. "Koda, once Celia starts removing whatever is lodged in there, the wolf's spirit will start to heal him. We'll have to keep the sides from closing. Otherwise, Celia will have to keep slicing him open."

"Got it," Koda replies. He casts Celia a nervous glance when she pales.

"You can do this," I tell her. "I know you can." I square my shoulders, gripping the wolf's lower limbs. "Ready?"

Celia nods.

Koda nods.

And Celia cuts.

It's a perfect incision. The wolf barely reacts. But when Celia reaches into the wolf's belly, it's another story entirely.

The wolf whines in agony. Gemini grunts, his head slamming back into the embankment. "Left, go left . . . there, down . . ." He roars. "Both hands . . .You have to use both hands . . ."

Celia's hands disappear deep beneath the flesh, her delicate features pinched.

"You have it," Gemini chokes. "That's it . . . . take it out . . . take it out, *now*."

Celia pulls on what can only be described as a sticky gray wasp's nest. I snag the wolf's limbs with one hand when it's halfway out and the skin begins to knit closed. Koda follows suit, giving Celia enough space to remove it and toss it away from us.

The clump of gray matter bursts open, releasing thousands of moths that take flight. I reach for Celia, dragging her behind me when Gemini's wolf breaks free from us.

Celia doesn't pay attention to the wolf, she'd too busy gaping at the moths as they disappear into the forest. "What was that?"

"Death," Koda says. For the first time since he met her, he smiles. "The same thing you saved our friend from."

She whips around, rushing to crouch beside Gemini. He's breathing hard and his skin shines with sweat. But with each breath he takes, his face resumes its normal healthy color. He smiles at Celia when his twin bounces to his side, wagging his tail. "Thank you for saving us," he whispers.

"I had help," she says, glancing away.

Celia rises, wiping her grimy hands against the sweatpants as she walks to where Liam lays silently.

"It's all right," Koda assures her. "That poison he swallowed didn't make it to his stomach. All you have to do is slit his throat and reach in . . .

The extraction went as easily as could be expected. Which is why I can't understand why Celia seems so, what's a good word here? Grossed out. Yeah, that works.

Sure, she had to shove her hand down the length of Liam's esophagus (Koda was a little off on where the lump of death was), and yeah, there was all the bile Liam spewed like a fountain. But he's fine now and there were way fewer moths than last time. Look at him, yapping away. He's as good as new.

"Celia, I'm never going to know what it's like to give birth," Liam tells her, making like she's not bent on all fours, working hard to breathe. "I don't have the parts, you hear what I'm saying? But I gotta tell ya, when your fist came out of the hole in my neck, holding that slimy, pulsating thing in your hand, it was everything I've ever imagined birth to be. You should have slapped that clump and gave it a name."

"Please stop speaking," she begs him.

He frowns. "Why? I'm just getting to the good part."

"Because she'll vomit," Koda snaps. "And die," he mutters to me.

"What?" I ask.

Koda shrugs. "Look at her, Aric. She can't heal and she's more human than beast."

"I don't know about that," I say, keeping my voice low.

"Didn't you say she couldn't even catch a fish?"

"Yeah," I begin.

"Ever hear of a cat who couldn't fish? Let alone a big cat? She's what you call delicate. Delicate beings throw up and die." He shakes his head. "It's a wonder she's made it this long. I mean, how many times have you heard about humans found dead, lying in their own vomit?"

"I see your point," I admit.

Gemini and his twin edge toward Celia. The twin whips his tail back and forth when he reaches Celia. Celia doesn't seem to notice, too busy scrubbing Liam's leftover bits from her arms in the river.

"That was some impressive surgery you performed," Gemini tells her.

Celia rubs her hands harder, the amount of dirt and fluid that caked her skin clouding the water. "I've watched a few operations online." She makes a face. "I'll be honest, it's easier to handle when you're not actually the one poking around."

Gemini smiles. "Are you planning on becoming a surgeon?"

She shakes out her hands, examining her fingernails closely. "No. I'm actually starting nursing school in another few weeks."

"Nursing school? Wait, how old are you?" I ask. I'm just suddenly there, although I didn't feel myself approach.

Celia tilts her head to better see me. It's more than she's done with my friends. "Fifteen," she replies.

"You're not in high school?"

She shakes out her hands and stands. "Not anymore. I dropped out and took my G.E.D."

"Why?" I ask.

Celia lowers her lashes, appearing not to want to say more. "My foster mother is really sick and she can't support us much longer. As the new head of the household, it's up to me to make sure we'll be okay." She lifts her chin. "It's one of the reasons I have to get back. They need me, Aric. They won't make it without me."

You're just a kid. I want to say. *Too young to have so much responsibility tossed on your shoulders.*

"I understand," I tell her. "But you can't go home. Not tonight. We don't know what's out there."

She wipes the remaining moisture on her shirt. "If I can just get to a bus or train station, I can get out of here. I'll take my chances. I've already been gone for too long."

"Celia, we can't let you leave on your own," I insist. "We just took on a skinwalker—a creature most are too terrified to speak of. He's not dead. Do you hear me? Even after everything we did to him, at best, he's vanquished. He could return, and this time with friends." I ignore Liam's shudder. "You're not safe out here, and you're definitely not safe on some bus. Come home with me and I promise to protect you."

"Aric," Koda begins.

"I'm not leaving her out here," I tell him.

"I'm not suggesting that," Koda says. "I wouldn't leave my worst enemy out here. Not after everything we went through. But you're a pure, Aric. It won't look good if the pack finds out you brought her home with you."

"My parents will understand," I insist.

It's true. But the rest of the pack won't.

Chapter Six

Celia wouldn't let me carry her, insisting she could manage. She slapped Liam's hands and growled when he tried to throw her over his shoulder. It was good for a laugh, and something we all needed given the day.

It's just about twilight when we reach the back of my property. We would have arrived faster, but Celia struggled to keep up in the sneakers Liam lent her. We shoved some moss inside and tied them tight, but her feet, like everything else, are tiny.

"Do you want us to walk you to the door?" Gemini asks. His twin should have returned to join his human counterpart, but like Gemini, he seems taken by Celia and doesn't appear to want to leave her. He sits beside her as I reach for the gate.

"We'll be okay," I say. "The wards should keep anything that threatens us out."

Koda cocks a thick brow. "Even a skinwalker?"

"Yeah," I say, although I'm no longer positive. The skinwalkers are the boogeymen of the supernatural realm, the ones who hide beneath your bed and stalk the woods after they kill you in your sleep.

I open the gate wide, giving Celia ample space. My friends wait until we step through, their shoulders sagging with relief when the wards don't disintegrate Celia into ash. I suppose it was the final test to prove she means me no harm. I wasn't worried. I've known that from the start.

Koda adjusts the elk he bagged against his shoulder. Gemini does, too. We nod our goodbyes before I click the gate shut and they turn away. Once we're in, Gemini's twin wolf leaps into Gem's bare back, dissolving like ink into a vat of clear water.

"Wow," Celia says.

"Yeah. Wow," I mutter.

I start toward the house, hoping she'll follow. "Does his twin ever turn human?"

I shake my head. "No. Gemini can become a wolf and divide in two like you just saw. But his twin is just another part of him. The theory is that his mother was carrying two babies, but only one survived and hung on to what remained of his twin's soul."

Celia smiles. "That's *amazing*."

It is. I've just known Gemini so long that I've accepted his ability as a part of him.

We start up the trail, wishing I could find the right words to say. I barely know anything about Celia, but what I do know makes me want to get to know her better. I only hope she wants to get to know me, too.

"What's wrong?" she asks.

"Nothing."

She nudges me with her elbow, the force hard enough to make me stumble. "What was that for?" I ask, laughing.

"Nothing," she says, smirking. "I'm sorry. Wasn't that what you just said to me?"

I chuckle. She can probably guess my mind is on other things. What she probably doesn't know is that those other things are her.

"Are you sure you're okay?" she asks.

"Yup. Just fine."

The large property darkens as we make our way toward the house and the breeze picks up, sprinkling pine needles from the overhanging branches onto our heads. Celia crosses her arms when the wind increases in speed and strips a few pine cones free of their posts. They thud against the ground like the small steps of a fawn the first time it runs. I've always enjoyed those gentle sounds. I suppose it's because they remind me of home.

"Are you cold?" I ask when Celia holds herself tighter.

"No. My tigress tends to keep me warm." She laughs a little. "Except last night was cold, and I can't maintain my form while I sleep."

"No?" I ask.

"Can you?"

"Always," I admit. "We camp out a lot. Sometimes, we don't even bring packs. It's just us, sleeping under the stars."

"That sounds nice."

I nod, mulling through what she said. "I don't mean to insult you, but I'm surprised by your tigress. I would think where your best interests are involved, she'd be there to help you out."

Celia quiets, keeping her attention ahead on where the well-worn path leads up to the barn. I start to think I went too far. But then she speaks in that cautious way she does when she's afraid to open up.

"Unlike your wolf, my tigress is almost a separate entity. She resides within me, but I'm not certain she shares my soul. You're better connected to your beast, from what I've seen. I'm not. There are moments when it's all I can do to keep her from wandering and under control."

"I don't know about that." I step ahead, lifting a low-lying branch to avoid it smacking me in the head. "When I'm angry or when I'm in danger like we were back on the mountain, my beast is quick to respond."

"Mine is, too," she admits. "But sometimes she responds in anger too quickly, making us do things that maybe we shouldn't."

"Like what?" I ask.

Her tigress eyes replace her own and she releases a shuddering breath. "Like hunt," she whispers.

The wind stills and the chirping birds settling into their nests appear to hunker down. "You don't mean game, do you?"

Her silence and the cool stare of her beast are answer enough.

"Does she make you do things you don't want to do?"

Celia opens her mouth, but then shuts it abruptly, continuing forward without me. It's not until the incline levels off that she realizes I'm not following.

This is a young, vulnerable girl who has suffered a great deal. I hate it, but I hate how it hurts her more.

"Celia?" I ask. "Does your tigress make you do things you don't want to do?"

Small tears form across her irises, dissolving the eyes of her tigress and returning those of the Celia I first met. She blinks, releasing them to cut lines down her dirty cheeks. "Yes," she admits. "It's how I think I got here."

I stop in front of her, fiddling with the strap of my pack. I'm not nervous. I'm scared. Scared for Celia and what's waiting for her at home. "What happened?"

"There were these men, who broke into our home when we were little. They killed my parents."

"Wow," I murmur, although the words that follow are harsher.

"I found those men. All of them. It took me several months, but I did it." She trembles. "I chased the last one down an alley. I had him, when something appeared several feet away."

"What was it?" I ask.

"I don't know. It was a dark figure. I could sense she meant me harm, and I felt her magic build when she saw me. But then something appeared behind *her*." She wipes her face, embarrassed by her openness. "The next thing I know, I woke up here with no clothes and no memory of how I arrived."

"I'm sorry," she says, when I don't respond. "I don't know why I'm telling you this. It's rare that I talk with anyone outside my family."

"Don't you have any friends?" Out of all the things I could have asked, I think this was possibly the worst.

"I have my sisters and Ana Lisa," she says, her tone even, despite how her expression flickers with sorrow no one this young should feel. "They're enough."

She swallows as hard as Liam did after she removed that clump of evil and his throat sealed shut. Just because she didn't ingest the poison he did, doesn't mean she hasn't felt her share of pain.

"I've said too much," she stammers. "I should go."

She doesn't quite turn around when I drop my pack and wrap my arms around her. My embrace isn't hard. It's a shelter from everything that hurts her, and a shield against anything that might try. I don't know Celia. We only met a few long hours ago. But everything I've seen makes up for it.

Celia faced an immense snarling wolf head on, telling him she didn't want to hurt him. She's a young woman who hid in embarrassment, but who took on a creature that *weres* live in fear of, knowing she couldn't heal if wounded.

This female saved my friends, my brothers, ignoring everything it could cost her.

No. I don't know Celia. But what I do know is enough.

That warmth amplifies between us, diffusing her fear and shame as if they never manifested. I bow my head, curling into her as her arms secure around my waist, the closeness we share reducing our intense breathing into something harmonious and calm.

"What are you doing to me?" she whispers.

I try to laugh. It doesn't quite come out. "I was going to ask you the same thing. You're like . . ."

"Magic?" she offers.

"Not quite." I nuzzle her closer, my jaw sweeping over her head. "You're peace."

"That's nice," she says. I release her when her arms slip away, even though neither of us seem ready to let go. "We could all use some peace."

The hoots from a distant owl is a firm reminder of how late it is. I offer Celia my hand, trying not to smile like a fool when she takes it. My dad always warned me that when I'd fall for a female, I'd fall hard. Still, I never pictured anything like this.

"Are you hungry?" She looks at me. "Sorry, that's a stupid question. We can talk things over with my folks while we eat. Mom always makes plenty of food."

"All right."

I give her hand a small squeeze. "What's wrong?"

"Aric, I know you mean well. But if your parents aren't okay with me staying, I understand. If I can just call home, Ana Lisa, my foster mother, will wire me the money to pay for the call and a ticket back home. Do you have access to Western Union or something like that?"

"We do, but it won't be necessary. My parents won't take a dime from you, and they'll welcome you like family."

"But they don't know me."

"True. But they know me, just like I know them. They're good people. Just make sure you eat plenty, otherwise you'll offend my Mom."

"I don't think you have to worry about that," she says. "I could eat a cow."

"Good," I say. "That's probably what's for dinner."

I pause when we come across a familiar spot. "Want to see something?"

"Is it evil?"

I bark out a laugh. "No. It's anything but."

"In that case, sure."

I lead her off the path until we're standing directly in front of a pine with a trunk as wide as my body. "Here," I say, guiding her around it.

She tilts her head when I point to the heart carved into the tree. "Who are A.C. and E.D.?" Celia asks, motioning to the initials.

"My parents, Aidan Connor and Eliza Dùghlas. They're mates," I add, when she glances back at me. "My father carved their initials into this tree the day they realized who they were to each other. My mother was so touched by the gesture, he bought this property to ensure nothing would ever happen to the tree."

"It was a wedding present," I say, when she continues to appear confused.

"What's a mate?"

I want to tell her it's a word connected to love, commitment, and honor. Stronger than marriage and the most sacred bond a *were* will ever share with another. But as I look into Celia's pretty face and see the way she patiently waits for me to explain—like I'm the only one who can explain it the right way—the words barely come.

"*Weres*, the lucky ones anyway, have mates," I say, my tone a whisper that vanishes in the increasing breeze. "That one special being they're destined to love and share a soul with for eternity."

Celia's gaze drifts to mine. "Do you think you'll have a mate someday?"

I think back to my parents, how lost they are when the other is not around, and how they cherish each smile and gentle touch. "I hope so," I rasp.

The wind picks up again, lifting Celia's long hair. It's similar to how it felt last night, the same kind of wind that brought me that dream. "I should get you inside," I tell her.

We hurry back onto the path and through the patch of woods that makes up most of our property.

The modern stone farmhouse my father built for my mother waits in darkness.

"Something's wrong," I say, moving faster.

"How do you know?" Celia asks.

"I don't know. It just is," I say, rushing forward.

I swing open the doors and hurry in. "You don't lock your doors?" Celia asks.

My pack drops to the floor as I kick off my shoes. "No. The wards surrounding the house are stronger than the ones along the perimeter."

I stop when Celia remains behind the threshold. "I don't know if I should come in. My feet are filthy."

Mud cakes them, and they're still a little bloody from her trek through the mountain. I could care less and so will my parents. I reach for her hand and help her inside. "It's all right," I assure her.

"Mom? Dad?" I call out.

Celia takes in the foyer, hugging herself. "Maybe they're not home. All the lights are out."

I wait and listen. "That doesn't mean anything. Sometimes, they're just upstairs having sex."

"Excuse me?"

When I don't hear them or anyone else, I pad into the kitchen, lifting the note my father left by the phone.

Aric,

Strange activity has been reported along the borders of Colorado. Witchcraft, very strong and unlike any we've seen, has stirred dark forces. Tornados and earthquakes are erupting all over the state.

Your mother and I are tasked with overseeing the packs prowling the affected areas and responding to reported threats in turn. *Call* when you arrive. The amount of magic used is greatly affecting the phone and power lines. Don't worry. We're fine, and all dark activity is occurring far from home.

~ Dad

"All dark activity is occurring far from home," I mutter. "Yeah. Sure it is."

Celia eases away from where she was reading the note. "What's happening?" she asks. "And why do I feel like I'm a part of it?"

There's nothing I'd like more than to assure her she has nothing to do with this mess. But the wind brought her here like Dorothy, and it threw the bogeymen and natural disasters across the Yellow Brick Road. "We'll figure it out," I promise her. "But first, I need to make a *call*."

Celia follows me to the rear doors leading out to the terrace. "I thought the phones aren't working?"

The wink and grin I cast her over my shoulder cause her to trip over her feet. "You'll see," I tell her.

The wind barrels through as we step onto the terrace, smacking hard against the side of the house. I press my hands against the dark wood railing and take a long deep breath, tapping into my inner beast.

I bow my spine and throw my head back, releasing a howl from deep in my soul, that primal place only *weres* and our ancestors have ever had the privilege of knowing. As I finish, I ease slowly forward, leaning my forearms against the railing.

The first to respond is my father, his deep baritone howl as familiar as his chuckle and quick wit. My mother follows, her howl lighter and as gentle and comforting as her touch.

Liam is next, his *call* ending with an excited yip. Gemini's ensues right after, his voice louder and clearer with the help of his twin. Koda is last, the mournful way his beast sings, and the direction his *call* comes from erasing my smile and alerting me he's home. He chose not to stay with our friends. Given what happened, I imagine he wanted to make certain his mother was safe.

I only wish she cared for his safety the same way.

The wind blows harder, this time against our faces. Celia's hair cascades behind her. Until now, I didn't realize her eyes were closed.

She opens them slowly. "That was beautiful," she says, her eyes sparkling against the pale moon. "How can your family hear you now, when they weren't able to before?"

"My parents and I share a stronger bond, because we're pures, and because they're mated. We also share a strong connection to our home and this land." I hadn't much thought about how special our family ties are until I explain them to Celia. The strong reminder of how lucky I am makes me smile. "On a clear day or night, they can hear me from hundreds of miles away."

"But not during earthquakes?" she guesses.

"No. Between the sound and the amount of magic used to create it, any *call* would be muffled."

"What about your friends?" she asks.

My fascination with Celia's beauty and subtle gestures make it hard to stay focused. I do my best. "My friends live close, so the distance and wind aren't an issue."

She nods, appearing to understand. She hesitates, then asks, "Is Koda okay? He sounded sad."

My loyalty to Koda won't allow me to say much. "He doesn't have it easy."

I gesture toward the house. "Come on. Let's get something to eat."

The refrigerator remained plenty cold when I opened it. I found the giant sides of beef Mom had prepared seasoned and ready to cook. I suppose I could have broiled them in the oven with just a strike of a match but chose instead to roast them over the firepit.

I beat back a grin when I caught Celia gaping at me as I chopped firewood. I was hot, sweaty, and shirtless. I pretended not to notice, and although I already had plenty of firewood by that point, I chopped some more.

Celia had drunk all the water we'd brought on the hunt. She drank even more as I cooked our meal. I was sure all that water would fill her and that she wouldn't be able to eat much. She surprised me by eating almost as much as I did. The meal made a big difference. She perked up and color returned to her cheeks.

I didn't want Celia to help me clean up. She did anyway and was as efficient and fast as my mother. I almost asked her if this was a regular task, but I didn't want to remind her of home, not when it would make her sad.

She washes the last dish and passes it to me to dry, covering her mouth to suppress a yawn.

"We should go to bed," I say.

Her eyes widen. "What?"

I don't have to look in the mirror to know my face is fire-engine red. "Ah, bed?" I repeat like a dumbass. "You know, in my room?"

Her tigress eyes replace her own. That's pretty much when I realize I'm in trouble. "I'm not going to bed with you."

My hands shoot out so fast, I almost break the plate when it lands on the counter. "That's not what I mean. I just want you *in* my bed."

"Oh, I bet you do," she snaps.

And that's when her claws come out.

"I mean, I want you in bed by yourself!" Holy crap, she looks ready to gut me. "Without me. Do you know what I'm saying?"

"*No.*"

Of course not. Celia doesn't speak moron. "You can stay in my room is all I meant." There. I said it. Why was that so hard?

Her nails slowly withdraw. "You want me to sleep in your bed?"

"Yes."

"By myself?" she clarifies.

Because I haven't looked like enough of an idiot, I click my tongue and make a little shooting motion with my fingers. "You got it."

She watches me for a beat, then another, her nails protruding and withdrawing again as if unsure whether to believe me or leave me a eunuch. "Where are you going to sleep?"

"I figured I'd sleep in the guestroom."

"You have a guestroom?" she asks.

"Yeah, a couple of them," I admit.

"But you want me in your room?"

"Ah, yeah."

Her claws are only a few inches out. This could be a good thing or a bad thing. She tilts her head. "Why shouldn't I take the guestroom? Or the couch? Or even the barn?"

How can I explain that I need her surrounded by my things, my scent? That only then will my wolf and I will feel she's safe. It's the same reason I gave her the shirt I was wearing earlier, instead of the clean one, and the reason my parents hold each other as much as they do. Our scents assure anyone who approaches that the other is spoken for and protected. I'm not saying Celia is spoken for by me, but maybe I'm saying I want her to be.

"My room has a full bathroom." I sigh. "And it looks like you really could use a shower."

Cue her blush.

And mine.

So help me, I wish I could kick my own ass.

I pinch the bridge of my nose. "I just figured you'll be more comfortable there. I'll just get my clothes out."

I can't get out of the kitchen fast enough. I race up the stairs and straight into my room. I pick up the dirty clothes on the floor and dump them in the second-floor laundry room. I hurry back and make my king-sized bed, turning the pillows this way and that until I'm sure I'm going insane.

With the exception of the stone brick wall where my headboard rests, my room is painted a slate blue. The floor has the same multi-colored wide wood planks in shades of gray, white, and brown as the rest of the house. Gray and rust-colored curtains hang over my large picture window, and a large gray comforter covers my bed. Aside from that, I have a desk, a dresser, and a nightstand.

I pick up the dark red pillows and switch them around again, placing them between the gray and blue ones.

"Do you need help?"

I grimace, wondering how long Celia has been watching me and praying it hasn't been long.

"You seem to be struggling with the pillows," she says, smiling. "Is this your first time making a bed?"

Great. She's been there a while. My only saving grace is that her claws aren't out, *yet*.

"It's just, you know," I mutter.

She crosses her arms and leans against the door frame. "No, I don't know. Please, enlighten me."

I toss the pillow I'm holding onto the bed and busy myself cranking the side window closed. It beats standing there like an imbecile waiting to make another dumb remark. "I just wanted things to be perfect, so you'll be comfortable."

"Oh," she says, no longer smiling.

Celia walks in slowly, passing her fingertips along the shelf that holds a few of my trophies. She pauses in front of the trophy I received for tracking, and the one beside it for wrestling. "These are nice," she says, smiling. "I'm very impressed by you."

She's impressed.

By me.

Yes!

I give my wolf a mental fist bump. "What about you? Do you play sports?"

Celia shakes her head. "No. I'm athletic, but I'm not really one to be a part of a team."

"Why? Too busy being homecoming queen or something?"

My grin fades at her frown. "Are you making fun of me?"

"Ah, no. I just figured someone like you would've been crowned prom princess or something."

"Someone like me?" she asks.

"Yeah. I mean you're pretty, have a great bod—personality, and you're nice. Real nice," I add when she just looks at me.

Celia steps away, appearing guarded. "Why don't you believe me?" I ask. "Can't you scent that I'm telling the truth?"

"Scent?" Her brows knit. "I don't understand what you mean."

I move closer, immediately stopping when she tenses. "Can't you smell a lie?"

"No," she replies. "Can you?"

"Yes," I tell her. "It's one of the first things we learn as *weres*."

"You forget, I wasn't raised around *weres*," she reminds me.

"It's not that," I say. "I just forget that your beast is different from mine."

Celia edges away when I approach, giving me plenty of space when I open my drawer. I pull out a T-shirt and a pair of cotton shorts and leave them folded on top of the dresser. I disappear into the bathroom and turn on the water. When I step back into my bedroom, I realize Celia hasn't moved.

"We have a tankless water heater," I explain, hooking my thumb in the direction of the bathroom. "It takes a moment for the water to heat, but once it does, you won't run out. I left you some towels, a toothbrush and everything you might need." I sigh, not wanting to leave her, but recognizing she needs privacy. "If you need anything, I'll be in the room next door."

I grab a pair of shorts and shoot out of the room, shutting the door behind me.

It takes all I have not to swear out loud. I wish I could have said more, or at least said enough to console her. Celia is a stranger in my house and in this state. There are scary monsters lurking around, and earthquakes and tornados striking without warning.

I press my forehead against the door, speaking low. "Goodnight, Celia."

I don't think she hears me, until her sweet voice whispers against the door. "Goodnight, Aric."

Chapter Seven

I moan, the soft cotton sheets sliding between my legs as I wrap my arms tighter around Celia.

Celia?

Oh, *no*.

We leap out of bed. The force she uses slamming her back against the wall. In my haste, I tangle the sheet around my ankle and fall on my ass.

"What are you doing in here?" she demands.

"Ah," is my response.

"Is that all you have to say for yourself?" she screeches.

My eyes widen when I realize she's not dressed. She's standing there, holding my comforter pressed against her barely covered breasts as her bed-tousled curls fall around her face. "I don't know."

"That's not much better," she snaps.

I yank my ankle free and stand. "I meant I don't know how I got here."

She looks to the window, then to the open bedroom door, then at me. "How did you get in here?"

"I have no idea," I reply. "I went to bed, I fell asleep, and that's all I remember."

My mouth stops moving when she bends to retrieve the clothes I gave her. They're torn as if ripped from her body. She lifts the pieces carefully and takes a sniff.

Anger darkens my tone. "I *did not* do that."

She lowers the torn fabric away from her nose, her expression pained. "I know."

"You do?"

"I did this to myself." Her gaze drifts to the opened door. "I think my tigress let you in."

I stare at the door, as if it can somehow clue me in to what happened.

"Aric, last night, after you left, I locked the door and shoved your dresser in front of it."

"Why?" It's stupid question, seeing how I woke up in bed next to her, but here I am, asking it anyway.

Her breathing slows, becoming more purposeful. "I was scared what you might do."

I'm already to her, clasping her bare shoulders gently. "I would *never* hurt you."

She nods like she believes me, despite the tears brimming in her eyes. I hold her carefully, trying to comfort her.

"No, *way*."

Liam's voice booms into the room. I whip around, growling and shielding Celia with my body.

"What?" Liam says, his elated smile immediately fading.

Koda stands behind him, his eyebrows practically to his hairline, while Gemini gapes back at me, shock and disappointment marching across his features.

"What are you doing here?" I snarl, menace stabbing each word.

Liam frowns. "We came by to help." He hops on top of my dresser and sits, swinging his legs like a little kid. "I was wracking my brain all night trying to figure out how to help Celia."

"And?" I ask.

"I've got nothin'.'" He shrugs. "I stopped at Koda's and Gem's on my way here to see if they had any ideas, but they don't have nothin', either. Hey, you have any food?"

"We should give Aric and Celia some space," Gemini says. He backs out of the room when he sees what's left of Celia's clothes. "We'll wait for you downstairs."

Koda follows without a word. Liam continues to sit there like he's waiting on the Tooth Fairy.

"Liam?" I say.

"Yeah?"

"*Go.*" Do I have to spell it out for him?

"Huh?" he asks. "Okay. I guess I can do that."

"And shut the door," I say, when he doesn't.

He jogs back to the door and shuts it, but not before giving us a big thumbs up.

Celia is officially the color of fire. "They think we .."

"Oh, yeah," I agree, pulling on a T-shirt. "I'll grab you something from my Mom's closet. She's bigger than you, but a lot smaller than me."

"Aric?" Celia's soft tone holds me in place. "You don't think we . . ."

My gaze melds with hers. "Trust me when I say I would have remembered that."

Her mouth pops open and she says nothing more. I head toward the door, my face growing hotter with each step. "I'll leave the clothes by the door. Come down when you're ready."

I pick out a blue cotton dress my mom gardens in for Celia. It's the one thing Mom wears that Celia won't have to roll up or risk tripping over. I leave it and the pack of Wonder Woman underwear I find, just outside my bedroom door.

Mom's always buying packs of socks and underwear to donate to women's shelters. I hope Celia doesn't take offense to it. I'd never want her to feel disrespected or uncomfortable.

I rub my face, trying to clear my head. I don't know how I ended up in Celia's bed or why her tigress allowed me in. It says a lot that her greatest protector would trust me and my wolf. Still, it scares the blazes out of me, too—no matter how much I loved waking up beside her.

Love?

Whoa.

I hop down the steps and into my family room. Koda is already going to town in the kitchen, making breakfast. It's the one meal we can all sort of cook.

Liam perks up when he sees me, lifting his hand in a high-five. "*My man.*"

"Ouch," he says, when I smack him upside the head.

"Not another word, Liam," I warn.

I throw open the door to the fridge and reach for the orange juice. Like everything else, it's still cold.

If Mom were home, she'd set the table all pretty and pour the juice into one of her flowery pitchers. I slam the plastic gallon of juice in the center of the table and place the plates, utensils, and a stack of napkins in a pile.

Gemini places five glasses on the table, his solemn expression snagging my attention.

"Can I talk to you outside?"

His voice is gruff, serious, bordering on melancholy. I shouldn't feel as guilty as I do, especially since I met Celia first. But Gem's been my best friend since we started grade school. He and his family had just moved here from Japan. Gemini didn't speak a word of English. But he knew how to play and that was good enough for me.

We walk out to the terrace in silence, but not before Koda shoots us a sharp look. He thinks we're about to throw down. I hope he's wrong.

I slam the door in Liam's face when he tries to follow. "You're only going to talk about this with Gemini?" he asks.

I almost answer yes. But I'm not sure I'm ready to tell Gemini what happened. He leans his back against the railing and crosses his arms. I assume the same pose I did last night when I stepped out here with Celia, leaning heavily on my forearms and looking out across the wooded property.

"Did you hurt her?" Gemini asks.

Fury should blind me. It doesn't. Not when his tone is this sad and quiet. "No."

"You were both ready and willing?" He shakes his head slowly when I don't answer. "You're young, Aric. For all we've talked about females and when we might pursue them, this seems too soon."

"That's 'cause it is," I agree. I'm not ready to have sex with anyone. Not even Celia.

He turns to face me. "We didn't do anything, Gemini. She locked the door to my bedroom, barricaded it to keep me out, and went to bed."

"Then why did we find you like we did?"

I shrug. "She thinks her tigress let me in."

"Let you in?" he asks. "Or your wolf?"

"That's a good question," I mumble, flicking an acorn from the railing. "I don't have to *change* to better connect with my wolf. Celia does." I crack my knuckles. "And from what she said, she can't maintain her tigress form while she sleeps."

"Then it was your beasts who connected. On a spiritual level," he clarifies when my eyes all but bulge from my head.

Gemini doesn't laugh much, but he does then. As our chuckles fade, his more serious persona returns. "I didn't really think you'd hurt her."

I smile without humor. "Then why'd you ask?"

"It didn't look good," he admits, brushing the brittle pine needles that litter the terrace with his foot. "I could sense her sadness long before we entered the room. And when I saw her clothes…" He sighs. "I *can't* let anything happen to her."

My spine stiffens and my wolf comes to full attention. "Look, I know you like her, but I won't hurt her or allow anyone else to."

The barest hint of a smile tugs at his lips. "It's not like that, Aric."

"Could have fooled me," I mutter.

He rubs his jaw, appearing to choose his words carefully. "This isn't going to make sense to you. I can barely make sense of it myself. But since I met Celia, I've been attracted to her."

"I've noticed," I reply, my tone sharper than I intend.

"Not like you are," he says, surprising me by staying relaxed. "I'm attracted to her, because of you."

"What does that even mean?"

"I'm not sure myself," he says, maintaining his composure. "It's as if my wolves and I have to keep her safe *for you*."

Now, I'm just confused. "You don't want her for yourself?" I ask.

"Like you do?" he asks, smiling. "No. And I think anyone who does would be foolish to try to take her from you."

I bow my head, ashamed of the way I treated my friend. "I'm not even sure Celia likes me."

"Trust me, Aric, she does." He clasps my shoulder. "Let's go inside and talk about what's next." His expression grows grim. "My parents left this morning to join the hunt. I didn't tell them about Celia."

I'm not surprised Gem kept quiet about Celia. He never runs his mouth about anything. And then there's Liam.

I think we're done until I catch his darkening expression. "Is there something you're not telling me?" I ask.

Gemini releases a weary breath. "The pack's been instructed to capture anything unusual and kill it if it fights back."

"They're assuming whatever they find might be the cause of the dark magic," I guess. Gem nods. "But Celia didn't cause any of it."

"I'm not saying she did. But darkness did accompany Celia's arrival. With skinwalkers and other malevolent entities rising, people and *weres* alike are scared. We need to be careful. When fear brews, wrong assumptions are made about those who are different."

And Celia is different.

We step inside. Liam and Celia stand quietly beside each other as Koda robotically serves eggs and leftover steak.

They heard the last bit of our conversation, at least where Celia is concerned.

Mom's dress is too big on her, but the color brightens her skin and eyes. She looks feminine, beautiful, and more vulnerable than I wish she was.

"We'll fix it," I say, not bothering to sugarcoat what we talked about.

"Yeah, we will," Liam agrees.

"Let's have breakfast first," Koda says, his shoulders strained.

We eat in silence. Aside from a few glances she shoots my way, Celia keeps her head down. She doesn't strike me as a shrinking violet, but I think if she had the choice, she'd leave now and not look back.

"I think I should leave."

I was right.

"No," we reply at once. Well, except for Liam, who is on his fourth round of eggs.

"Celia, we're young and strong," Koda says. "We've been trained to hunt and kill and bring our opponent down." He pauses. "We had our asses handed to us yesterday. Five of us plus Gemini's wolf and we barely made it out alive. From what I heard in town this morning, these things are everywhere." He stabs a piece of steak and lifts it to his mouth. "No way would you stand a chance on your own."

Liam jumps to his feet, the motion so fast his chair topples over and slams onto the floor. "Magic," he says. "This whole thing is about magic." He points at Celia. "I say we take her to Mimi."

The wolves and I toss our forks, groaning, Gemini going as far as covering his face.

Celia blinks back at our sour expressions. "Who's Mimi?"

"Only the greatest hag you'll ever find," Liam says over Koda's, "Liam's nutso aunt," explanation.

"She's not nutso," Liam fires back. "She's just a little eccentric."

"Eccentric means you act a little funny or maybe dress up in that cosplay crap," Koda says. "Eccentric doesn't mean you blow up anyone stupid enough to knock on your door."

Liam bats his hands. "That was just the one time," he says. "And your hair grew back just fine. Besides, I told you she's hard of hearing. She wouldn't have zapped you like she did if you'd spoken up."

Liam's explanation does nothing to ease Celia's worry. "What is she, exactly?"

Liam frowns. "I told you. The greatest hag ever."

He sniffs the air, tilting his head from side to side when he detects Celia's confusion.

"You don't know what a hag is, do you?" I ask.

"Sure, she does," Liam answers for her.

Gemini eyes Celia carefully. "If she does, it's only from lore, not our world."

He keeps his voice gentle. I appreciate it more than I can say. Celia is anxious and worried about her family. Her arrival makes no sense and like Dad said, there was a large amount of magic the night she materialized in the woods.

Liam flips over the chair, straddling it and giving Celia the onceover. "You seriously aren't familiar with hags?"

"I assume you mean some kind of witch?" she asks me.

"Yes," I reply. "I think what you saw right before you disappeared was a witch—or some kind of spell wielder." I motion to Liam with a tilt of my chin. "Like Liam figured, to deal with magic, we have to go to someone who knows it well. Hags, like witches, are born with their power. But they tend to be . . ." Psycho is the first word that comes to mind. I don't say it because Mimi is Liam's aunt. "What I mean is, they're a little . . ."

"Eccentric," Liam offers, as if I missed his word choice the first time.

"Mischievous," I offer, instead. It's the most polite way to describe hags, especially Liam's bat-shit-crazy relative.

"That's one way to put it," Koda mutters. He props an elbow on the table and turns to me. "Can you *call* Bellissima?"

"Oh! Or her daughter, Genevieve," Liam suggests. "She's hot."

"Liam, put a sock in it," Koda tells him. He motions to me. "Well, can you?"

"I'm not authorized," I tell him.

"Then her daughter, Genevieve, like Liam said."

"Koda, powerful or not, she's too young," I remind him. "Plus, everything she does has to go through her mother first."

"It's protocol," Gemini agrees. "Aric would be crossing a line and we would be risking exposing Celia. Mimi is many things, but she won't report Celia."

"Are you sure?" Celia asks.

"She has no ties or loyalty to anyone," I assure her, casting a glance at Liam. "Except maybe family."

Koda tosses his napkin aside. "Can't you think of something else? *Anything else*?" He spits out a curse. "Tell me you're not seriously thinking about visiting Mimi?"

"What choice do we have?" I ask. "I can't call the head witch without breaking protocol, or handing Celia over. Another strong and sane witch—"

"Sane being the right word," Koda mumbles.

"May be willing to help," I continue, ignoring him. "But they have no loyalty to us and even if we could trust them, they've likely been called upon to deal with the rising darkness."

"You seem really hesitant about reaching out to Liam's aunt," Celia points out.

"Oh, yeah," the rest of us collectively mumble.

"Why?" Celia presses.

Gemini leans toward Celia, keeping enough distance so as not to crowd her. "Think of hags as the tricksters in the supernatural world," he explains. "Their tendency toward rebellion and mischief ostracizes them from coven witches, who commit to their craft."

Liam scratches his head, pulling out what looks like a spider and sniffing it before tossing it aside. "In other words, a little eccentric, like I mentioned the first time."

"Is she dangerous?" Celia asks.

Liam laughs. "Totally." He nudges Koda. "Remember that werecougar she turned inside out for stealing her tomatoes?"

Koda's brows leap up to his hairline. "That was her? I thought it was one of those stories parents tell their kids to warn them away from hags." He motions to Celia, whose eyes are practically shooting out of her head. "If that was Mimi's doing, what's she going to do to something like Celia? Cast a spell so her tongue slithers from her mouth and chokes her to death? Give her bellybutton fangs and make it devour her?"

"Enough," I say, practically snapping my teeth. "We get the point."

Gemini is pinching the bridge of his nose so hard, he's close to cracking the bone. "None of this is helping."

Koda glowers, insulted. "Mimi is unpredictable on a good day. Murderous on a bad. Fear brings out the crazy in crazies. If Mimi sees Celia as a threat, she'll feed Celia her eyeballs or worse."

Celia holds out a hand. "I'm going to stop you right there."

What little patience I have left reflects in my stance. "Celia, Mimi is a lot of things. But she's not cruel."

"She turned some cougar inside out," Celia reminds me. "What do call that?"

"Vengeance," Liam says. "He did steal her tomatoes. Are you going to steal her tomatoes?" Liam's grin lights up the room when Celia shakes her head. "Then what's the problem?"

I reach for Celia's hand, scrunching my face tight to prevent the shudder that the skin on skin contact creates. It doesn't work, and my friends take notice.

Koda's eyes shift from side to side as if unsure where to look. Gemini edges further away, noting the gentle way I hold her. Liam gives me a "*Nice*" and offers me a fist bump. I may have to kill them later.

I ignore them, focusing on Celia. "I know you're hesitant about approaching supernaturals." My glare trains briefly on Liam. "Not that I blame you. But as much as Mimi isn't my first choice, she's powerful and wicked smart. If anyone can figure out how you arrived and how to get you back, it's her."

Celia seems torn. "Look. I know you're trying to help. But . . ."

"But what?" I press, stroking her hand with my thumb when she doesn't answer.

"I don't belong here."

"In Colorado?" Liam asks. "We know that, Celia."

"I mean as part of your world." Her eyes glisten with fear. "My sisters and I have spent our entire lives avoiding the mystical community. We don't want any part of it. Now, you're asking me to stay and seek a being who may or may not kill me, just because I'm different."

"She won't kill you," I tell her. "I promise."

"Yeah," Liam agrees. "She may just slap you around a little bit." He holds up his hands. "I mean that in a purely magical sense."

"*Liam*," Koda snarls. He knows I'm seconds from losing it. "Stop trying to help."

"Aric, please," Celia says. "I know you don't know me, but if you could just lend me the money to get a bus back to Jersey, I promise I'll pay you back." Her expression steels, as if seconds from bolting. "I know very little about magic. What I do know has harmed me and my family beyond repair. I have to get back to them. They need me. Do you understand? I'm the only one who can protect them."

My hand squeezes hers, trying to soothe her beast and mine. My wolf yelps nervously, urging me to stop her from leaving us. He doesn't want her to go, and he recognizes the danger she's in.

I wrestle with what to do. Maybe I should buy a bus ticket. Maybe I should buy two. I can go with her to make sure she gets home safe.

I release her hand when my wolf howls a warning. "Celia, something magical put you here. Sending you back to Jersey will be like sending you back to whatever targeted you."

"You don't know that. But say you're right. If it came after me, it may go after my family." She stands. "I won't let anything happen to them."

"Neither will I," I say, trying to sound reasonable and to keep my wolf in check. "I know you're scared, and that you don't have a lot of faith in us." I sigh when Liam asks me to pass the bacon. "But you're in danger." I glance at my friends. "And unless we can figure this out, so is the rest of our pack."

Chapter Eight

I knew Celia was fast. The way she outran me yesterday blew me away. How she avoided falling to her death when the earth collapsed beneath her feet was something to see. But as fast as she was, I didn't expect her endurance to rival mine. I don't know much about tigers, but I know they can't maintain their maximum speed for long. Celia does just fine, keeping pace, despite the fact that her legs are nowhere near as long as ours.

We jet through the rough terrain leading to Mimi's territory, avoiding the dense tree trunks and rows of brambles with ease. Our feet barely make a sound as they push into the earth and kick up debris. I'm quiet when I move. Celia is close to silent, disappearing into her environment as naturally as her inner beast.

Gemini carries the elk he bagged yesterday in a fireman's carry. He's gifting it to Mimi as payment for her knowledge. Koda offered his elk, as well, but I refused. He needs it. If Mimi requires more as an offering, I'll think of something else.

"Does he need help?" Celia asks, glancing behind her toward Gemini.

Gemini is breathing harder, because of the weight of his kill. Still, if he had to, he could run the rest of the day and into the night. Celia doesn't seem to know that. She doesn't know a lot of things, which worries me. As much as she's avoided the mystical world, it seems to have its eyes set on her.

"He's fine," I say, keeping my voice low.

"Are you sure?" she asks. "I'm happy to take over."

"I know you're trying to be nice, but an offer of help would be construed as an insult and make Gemini appear weak."

"Because I'm a girl?" she asks.

She's not being defensive. She's curious and trying to understand. It makes it hard to say what I do. "No. Because you're not one of us."

Celia doesn't like what I have to say, but neither her steps nor her voice falters. "I know."

"That's not what I mean." I'm so preoccupied with her that I misjudge the set of boulders we encounter and stumble as I land. My hiking boots slide across the soil and I barely keep my feet.

Gemini's twin wolf tosses me a look over his shoulder. He knows I don't fall, ever. But I also don't encounter females like Celia.

Like Gemini's twin, Celia doesn't miss my almost wipe-out. It bruises my pride more than it should. I stumble over my words like I did my landing.

"I don't mean to offend you," I press, trying to normalize my breathing and beat away the flush of heat overtaking my face. "I'm just trying to make you understand our ways."

She keeps her focus ahead, saving her words until we leap over the next set of boulders. These are sharper and more jagged than the last. I need to concentrate to avoid an injury that could slow us down.

"Understand your ways?" she repeats, maneuvering over the boulders as easily as she did flat land. "So, I don't say something that will make me get zapped inside out?"

She's trying to make a joke. I manage a grin. "No," I say, catching her pretty face in my periphery. "I just want you to know more about me, so maybe I can know more about you."

Her surprise is as clear as the mountain air surrounding us. I'm stunned. Back in *Jersey*, there has to be an army of males trying to get with her—telling her how beautiful she is, wanting to spend time with her, and—

"Is something wrong?" she asks. "You look ready to chew on someone's jugular." She looks ahead as if danger lurks around the next cluster of trees.

I clear my throat, a stupid habit I've developed since I met her. It doesn't, however, clear the thoughts of all the males who are no-doubt pacing and panting in anticipation of Celia's return.

"I'm good," I reply.

Liam speeds up to run beside me. "Hey, Aric. Are you blushing?"

"No," I say through my teeth. "I'm just hot from running."

Celia can't sniff a lie. Liam can. He throws back his head, laughing. "Liar. You are blushing. Is it because of Celia?" If that's not bad enough, he points. "Hey, Koda. Aric's blushing in front of Celia again. You're right, he has it bad—oh, look! She's blushing, too. You totally have to see it—"

I shoot my foot out, hooking his ankle and making him fall on his face. Liam scrambles to his feet, spitting out dirt. "What was that for?"

"Sorry, that was an accident," I say, lying again.

I reduce my pace and hold out an arm as we near Mimi's territory. "We're here," I say. "Let's take things slow."

Gemini's twin wolf stops a few paces in front of us. He whines, his dark eyes peering ahead. He's about excited to visit Mimi as the rest of us.

"Watch," Gemini tells him.

The wolf takes point beside the elk as Gemini lowers it to the ground. "I feel bad that you have to do this," Celia tells Gemini. "I'm not sure when or how, but I promise to make it up to."

Gemini turns away, embarrassed. I can't blame him. Out of all of us, he's the most quiet and shy around females, especially cute ones. Except Celia isn't one of those cute types, those who know they're cute and who toss their hair to get attention.

Celia is muddy. Her skin glistens from the run and she's covered with cuts and scratches.

She's also the most beautiful girl I've ever seen.

"You owe me nothing," Gemini says. "Just stay safe."

She watches him. "I wish you could meet my sister, Taran."

Gemini perks up. "Why? Is she pretty?" he blurts out.

This time, I'm not the one blushing.

"She's gorgeous," Celia cautiously replies, but then she laughs. "She's also mouthy, loud, temperamental, and completely inappropriate."

Gemini cocks his head. "That doesn't sound like anyone I'd be attracted to."

"I don't know about that," Celia muses. "What I do know is Taran would make you smile. I think you could use a few more smiles."

She eases away from him and closer to me, looking in the direction where the trees thin to reveal a small worn path. "That's the way to Mimi's home?" she asks.

"It is," I reply. My wolf is on edge, his jaws firmly shut and his keen senses surging mine further.

I reach for Celia's hand and lead her forward. "Come on. The sky is getting darker and Mimi's vision isn't the best. The last thing I want is for her to think this is an ambush."

Celia's focus flickers back to where Gemini's twin waits beside the elk. "Will he be all right without us?"

"He'll be fine," Gemini assures her. He takes point behind us, not bothering to explain that the wolf won't just guard Mimi's payment. He's our back up and who we're counting on to warn us if something else appears.

I ease Celia behind me when we reach the path. "Step where I step," I tell her.

"Take nothing from Mimi, not even a blade of grass," Gemini warns.

"If she offers you something, wait for our signal before you ingest it," Koda rumbles.

The path opens up to a misshapen clearing, roughly the size of an acre. My mother's garden is neat and tidy, made up of rows of raised planter boxes Dad and I constructed throughout the years. Herbs line one side, vegetables the others, the entire section covered with carefully fastened wire to keep animals out.

Mimi has two gardens on either side of us. Each look like the equivalent of a toddler's bedroom following a vicious tantrum, except, instead of toys, waist-high plants spring up between tall sections of weeds and grass.

Liam prowls forward like it's a walk through a field of daisies and not some crazy hag's much-guarded territory. "You guys are making too much of a big deal out of this," he says. "Mimi isn't that bad. Besides, I'm her favorite."

Koda rolls his eyes as he takes point beside me. Liam thinks he's everyone's favorite. Stupid and often asinine comments aside, Liam *is* a good guy. If he could just keep his trap shut, he'd make great strides in the *were* community. The problem is, Liam can't zip it, and we usually end up in trouble because of him.

Liam turns around, grinning ear to ear when he sees me reach for Celia's hand. "So, are you two a thing? Or are you just using each other for a few kisses and cuddles?"

Did I mention Liam can't keep his trap shut?

I keep my features locked on him as my face goes up in flames. "We just met," I remind him.

Liam laughs. "You'd never know it, Juliette."

He means Romeo, but I'm not going there with Liam. I'm just hoping he won't mention marriage and making babies next.

"Just ignore him," I grumble. I shoot forward, pausing when Celia hesitates. Her fingers slip away from mine. I think Liam scared her off. But just as they near the pads of my fingers, she slides them back within my hold.

I squeeze her hand to reassure her. It's something Dad does with Mom. Mom seems to like it. I hope Celia does, too.

She glances down, as if ready to run the other way and all the way back to Jersey. But then she looks up and smiles, and all sorts of feelings melt my insides.

"Are you guys going to be bed buddies again tonight? Do you think your parents will mind? If they don't, could you tell them to talk to mine? I'd like a bed buddy. Wouldn't you, Koda?"

Only Liam can kill a moment like this.

Another wave of heat prickles my cheeks. Liam sticking his foot in his mouth is usually good for a laugh. Not now. The good thing is that it usually only takes something shiny to distract him.

Today, that shiny something is the sum of Mimi's power.

Like a strong wind, it comes at us from all sides, surrounding us.

"Don't move," I tell Celia. My voice cuts off when the magic pokes at me like a long, crooked finger. It's not aggressive, but it is a warning against moving or starting trouble.

I try to get a handle on where Mimi might be. I sense her magic all around us, on the ground, in the plants, and all the way up to the darkening clouds. But while I feel her power, I don't actually feel Mimi.

"Something's touching me," Celia say, her raspy voice close to a growl.

"It's Mimi's magic," I explain. "It's trying to determine if we're friend or foe."

Celia swallows back a growl. "What happens if she thinks we're foe?"

It's Liam, the ray of sunshine, who answers. "Oh, then we're totally screwed."

"Is she close?" Celia asks.

I reach out with my senses, taking care to appear unthreatening as the magic continues to prod. "I'm not sure yet. This is more akin to a security system, meant to keep the bad guys out."

"And blast anyone she doesn't like into oblivion," Liam adds. "Oh, look. Tomatoes."

"Touch those tomatoes and I'll tear your fucking liver out," Koda snarls.

Gemini inches closer to Celia. "I know you're scared," he tells her. "But try to relax so the spell doesn't misinterpret your fear for danger."

"I'm trying," Celia says, her breath releasing in quick bursts. "But my tigress wants out and I'm having trouble controlling her."

"Did you say you're having trouble controlling your inner beast?" Liam yells. "That big tiger with the huge claws?"

By now, even Gemini is ready to knock him unconscious. *"Yes, Liam."*

Celia's breathing harder than she did when she ran. "I'm not sure if I can keep her in."

I tuck her against me, speaking quietly. "Baby, you have to. I swear, I won't let anything happen to you, and my wolf won't let anything happen to your tigress."

"Baby." It's not what I meant to call her, but it's exactly what came out. Had it been Koda, Gemini, or even Liam who referred to a female that way, I would have laughed in his face and thought he's an idiot. But it's me and no one is laughing.

I expect a jab thrown my way, or at the very least a few eye rolls. Aside from saying hi and offering the occasional wave, I don't know how to communicate with girls and I've never really tried. It doesn't matter. What I said is enough.

Celia lowers her eyelids, her breathing slowing. It takes a moment for her to open them again, but when she does, she appears in control.

I relax and so does my wolf.

"Aric," Koda says, taking a cautious step forward. "I think Mimi's inside her house."

He motions ahead, where an old battered door covers the mouth of a cave, the warped wood it's made from barely clinging to the rusty hinges.

"She lives in a cave?" Celia asks, her focus sharp as she waits for my answer.

Around Celia, words don't come as easily as I'd like. Liam beats me to the punch. "Totally. Mimi loves caves."

"Why?" Celia questions.

Liam prowls ahead. "My family is a mix of *weres* and humans," he says. "Every few centuries, all the human and *were* breeding results in a witch. We hadn't had a witch for almost three centuries before we got lucky and Mimi came along."

"Yeah, lucky," Koda mutters.

"That doesn't explain why she lives in a cave," Celia reminds him.

"Oh, yeah," Liam says. "You did say something about that. Mimi was really fond of her grandfather, a werebear." He laughs. "Don't ask me how that happened, seeing most of us are wolves. But I hear my great-great aunt was kind of trampy."

"Language," Gemini says, looking at Celia.

"Sorry, Celia," Liam offers. "That means she slept around a lot."

A smirk forms on Celia's lips. "I know what it means, Liam."

Liam is halfway to the cave and unharmed. I look up at the darkening sky. I don't want to run back through the woods in the rain. Celia will get soaked and, like Koda says, humans are delicate and a cold might kill her.

"We're running out of time," I say. "Let's see if she's here so we can get this over with."

Liam bounds forward. His heart is so big he often forgets to be cautious when he's around those he supposedly knows. I should remind him, but I don't want to embarrass him.

"I still don't understand why Mimi lives in a cave," Celia says, keeping her voice soft so only I hear her. "Is it to honor her grandfather?"

Knowing she only means to speak to me makes me smile. "Mimi may be a hag, but she identifies more with the *were* side, because of our magic."

"I see," she says, appearing troubled.

"What's wrong?" I ask, taking a careful step around what resembles a patch of berries.

"Liam has *were* and human in his blood."

"That's right," I reply.

"How? Most of the humans I know are oblivious to the supernatural world."

"The majority are. But in states where wildlife continues to thrive, you'll find large populations of *weres* who've mated with humans. The magic we carry prevents non-*were* family members from sharing our secrets."

I stop in front of what looks like a large pumpkin vine. If pumpkin vines had thorns.

"That wasn't there before," I say.

"No, it wasn't," Celia agrees.

"Neither was that," Koda says.

He points to a bush spilling with raspberries the size of apples. The breeze picks up, causing one to break off from the branch and smash against the ground. It splatters like blood, soaking the dirt.

A small whimper echoes from deep within the soil. Our eyes widen and we back away from the bush.

"Tell me Mimi's magic didn't just make *dirt* cry," Koda says. He scowls when no one answers. "Are you kidding me right now?"

"Keep your voice down," I warn. Celia just reined in her tigress. The last thing I want is for Koda's wolf to lose it, too.

Another wave of magic pummels us, this time stronger, turning pokes and prods into outright shoves.

"She thinks I'm here to hurt her," Celia says, shaking violently when more of Mimi's energy surges.

I want to reassure her and Koda. For someone who should have control over his beast, Koda's big red wolf is seconds from unraveling. But then Mimi's magic smacks me across the face like an insolent brat, pissing me and my wolf off.

Gemini is shaking violently. Like the rest of us, he's barely curbing his primal side. From far behind us, his twin howls, beckoning us to return.

Almost at once, the path leading to Mimi's cave narrows. The tomatoes, the ones the size of watermelons dangling from flimsy shoots, the same ones we've tried to avoid, close in.

Celia inches away from the tomatoes. So do I. So does Gemini and Koda. *Weres* are capable of many things. Reversing spells that turn us inside out are not among them.

Another current of power branches up and out of the earth like a twisting beanstalk.

If beanstalks sprouted needles and spit fire.

Koda yelps and hops away, the hem of his jeans singed. His glare sweeps to the spot where he just stood. There's nothing there, but whatever it is, it's *everywhere*.

My hand tightens around Celia's. "We have to get out of here," I say, trying to keep my voice calm. My wolf paces restlessly, demanding out. "Walk slowly and retrace your steps as best you can."

Everyone nods and we begin to retreat.

Everyone except Liam.

I jerk my head when I realize Liam didn't so much as pause. He lifts his hand, ready to knock on Mimi's door.

"Liam, stop!" I yell.

Liam glances over his shoulder, appearing annoyed. "You guys are acting like a bunch of pussies. No offense, Celia. Let's take care of business so we can get out of here. I'm hungry."

It's the last thing he says before an explosion of black and gray magic slings us back like pebbles thrown across a lake.

A lake swarming with chaos and magic.

Chapter Nine

Mimi's magic blinds me. It blinds everything, turning the entire area into a disorienting cloud of light and sound. Time slows as I soar, spinning into the air, my over-stimulated senses shoving me toward mental collapse. Noise batters my eardrums and odd vibrations grate and twist my skin, while tinny and deep bellowing echoes pelt my skull like pounds of falling hail.

The spell is strong. I can taste it; a mixture of warm, curdling milk and rotting lemons thick enough to coat my tongue. I can smell it, too, my eyes watering as it singes through my nose.

Mimi's power is meant to confuse and overcome trespassers.

It does a good job.

My instincts take over as Celia slips from my grasp. I yank her against me, clutching her body and shielding her head. She falls on top of me as my body crashes into the earth like a meteor.

The sheer force of Mimi's spell drags me against the dank soil, creating a thick groove and partially burying us. I cough, gasping for air.

Celia coughs, too, but her breathing appears less harsh. Her hands fall on either side of my head. "Are you all right?' she asks. "Aric, can you hear me?"

Her voice sounds muffled. I think my hearing is damaged from the spell until Celia straddles me and hauls me into a sitting position. With a crackle and several pops, clumps of dirt spill from my hair and ears and fall against my shoulders.

"I'm fine," I say, shaking my head to clear what remains. "You?"

"I'm all right," she says. "Just a little banged up."

Very slowly, the cloud of dirt, dust, and whatever Mimi packed into that spell clears. Celia rests on my lap, her body angled toward the opening of the large hole I created. "We need to get out here," she whispers. "I don't feel her, but I don't want to set off another magical boobytrap."

"Tell me about it." My hand rests on Celia's thigh. I give it a squeeze. "Stay close. Okay? I don't want anything to happen to you."

She tilts her head to the side, her gaze fastening on mine. It holds like a formidable force, sending my heartbeat racing full speed ahead. I open my mouth to say something. But the words don't come. Not then. She lifts her hand to my cheek, carefully brushing away a spot of dirt. The motion is so soothing, I forget where I am.

Her voice is barely a breath of sound. "I don't want anything to happen to you, either."

"That's my job," I mumble.

"What?"

"Me protecting you," I explain. "That's my job, because you're a girl and . . . stuff."

My idiotic response goes over as well as you think.

Her hand falls away. "Are you calling me weak?"

"No, not weak," I quickly say. "Just, you know, delicate."

"Aric, call me delicate one more time and I'll leave you buried in this stupid hole."

She's pissed, insulted, and everything she deserves to be. And here I am, smirking and barely able to hold back a laugh. "Is now a good time to tell you I'm not good with girls?"

"You don't have to." She pats my arm. "It shows, big guy."

Celia shifts her weight, sliding off me and allowing me to ease into a crouch. We poke our heads out, scanning the area for any signs of mystical energy. There are none. This spell—trap—whatever it was, seems to have a one-time activation switch. Not that it needed more than that.

Koda rises from the demolished shed he crashed into, cursing when he glances at his shoulder. He removes a sharp piece of wood imbedded in his muscle, and a nail that pierced straight through his palm.

Gemini staggers from the direction of the forest, having been thrown further back than the rest of us. Pine needles and dirt coat his hair and body. He appears slightly disoriented, but he is otherwise unharmed.

We discreetly slip out, moving soundlessly toward Koda just as Gemini reaches him.

Celia stops dead. I whip around to see what's keeping her, worried another booby trap is set to go off.

She doesn't move. She doesn't even breathe, her attention fixed to our far left, where a sneaker lies discarded, the laces smoking.

"Aric?" she says. "Is that Liam's shoe?"

Five sets of curses fly out of Koda's mouth as he shoots forward. Gemini tears after him. It takes me a second to realize they're racing toward the opposite end of the demolished garden where Liam's *feet* are sticking up from the ground, flailing.

I make it to Liam with Celia close at my heels. Koda snags one leg and Gemini the other, pulling hard.

Liam pops out, like lettuce being torn from the ground. He's breathing, but that's about it. His clothes are in tatters and his chest is covered with dirt, bright red blood, and what smells like soot. Koda and Gemini try to steady him, but it takes some doing, given that Liam's head is twisted at an odd angle and his face is resting between his shoulder blades.

It's safe to say Celia doesn't like what she sees.

She covers her mouth with one hand and slaps my arm blindly with the other. "Oh, my God," she says. "Oh, my God. Oh, *my God*."

I place my hand on her shoulder. "It's okay. These things happen."

Celia veers toward me. "These things happen? No—*no*. You can use that line when people trip over a cracked sidewalk or misplace a few dollars. You can't say something like that when they have their heads twisted like corkscrews and eyes dangling down their backs. I mean, *come on*, Aric. Liam didn't even touch her tomatoes!"

Liam continues to flail. For someone like Celia who's not used to beings like us, I suppose this looks bad. "He'll be all right," I assure her. "See? That eye that launched out of his socket is already making its way back into his skull." I realize I'm not making her feel better when her skin whitens to ash. "He's a *were*. He'll be as good as new in no time."

"My ass!" Liam screams. "Why am I looking at my ass?"

"Your psycho aunt's magic snapped your neck around," Koda says. "Keep still so Gemini can crack it back into place before the bone heals."

Celia's jaw falls open with an audible pop. "The bone can heal that way?" she asks. "Permanently?"

"Sure. Our inner beasts repair our bodies when broken," I explain. "But they don't always know to align them or to return them to a specific direction. Gemini will have to break his neck first and—"

"Oh, *God*," Celia says.

"I notice you talk to God a lot," Liam points out, his hands and feet moving in the opposite direction he likely intends. "She's a nice religious girl, Aric. Your mom will like that."

If Liam could see the shade of green Celia's skin has taken, I'd think he'd filter his remarks. Never mind. This is Liam I'm talking about.

"Liam, you have to stop moving, bruh," Koda tells him.

"Can't help it," Liam says. "My wolf is getting restless."

"I'll help," Koda says. "Just don't bite me like last time."

"Like last time," Celia says, speaking slowly. "Of course there was a last time."

"Make it fast," I call out, scanning the area and beyond. "Mimi isn't here, but she also isn't far. I don't want to be here when she returns and she sees her yard blown to bits."

"No, kidding," Koda mutters. He lifts Liam in a bear hug, securing his arms against his sides. "You ready?" he asks Gemini.

Gemini doesn't answer, rubbing his chin and scrutinizing the shape of Liam's neck. "I don't know."

"What do you mean you don't know?" Koda demands. "He looks like a freak of nature."

"No offense, Celia," Liam calls out.

I roll my eyes, wondering how I haven't kicked Liam's ass yet. "What's the problem, Gem?" I ask.

Gemini turns Liam's head from side to side. "The break set at an angle. I think Liam's wolf grew another vertebra to secure the position. If so, I have to break it off first, then quickly break his neck again before we end up with more pieces."

"Can't we just jam his head in place and tear off the bones he doesn't need?" Koda suggests.

Celia is no longer talking to God. She's not talking at all, which worries me more.

"Are you messin' with me?" Liam asks. "This freakin' hurts. And now you're talking about ripping out the extra stuff my wolf took the time to grow? You guys suck."

They start arguing among themselves like little kids on the playground, instead of the Guardians of the Earth we pride ourselves to be. I'm not embarrassed on behalf of our kind or anything. No. Not at all.

"Do they know what they're doing?" Celia asks, swallowing hard between words. "It doesn't sound like they know what to do."

"They're fine," I insist. "One time, we were wrestling, and my elbow popped free of the joint." I point to it. "It was a good break, but not a clean one. The sharp piece of bone pierced through my skin and Gemini had to poke it back in place." I lift my arm higher. "See, it worked out in the end and he didn't even have to wash his hands before doing it."

Celia meets me square in the eye. "I think I might actually vomit."

I frown. "Don't do that. You'll get dehydrated and die."

Celia isn't a fan of my logic. I'll have to work on it, if she's going to be my girlfriend like I want her to be. She jumps when Gemini grabs Liam's head and twists, the cracking sound ricocheting across the garden like a bag of chips being smashed.

"The other way," Liam says, spitting the words out through his teeth. "You're going right and you need to go left."

"I'm going the right way," Gemini argues. "You just don't know it."

"I do so know it," Liam insists. "Just like I know you're one twist away from ripping my head off!"

"Liam, cut it out!" Koda snarls when Liam kicks him. "It's gonna end up all twisted if you don't stop."

"Left. Go left!" Liam hollers.

"You don't get it," Gemini explains. He keeps his cool, but Gem's like that. "Whatever Mimi did twisted your neck twice in a row. You're lucky your spine didn't rupture through the skin."

"Oh," Liam says. "That makes more sense. Just hurry up. My wolf is ready to sink his fangs into your throats and spit out your larynxes."

One crunch follows three snaps with a crack in between. It takes some doing on Gem's part, until Liam's head is square on his shoulders where it belongs. His neck is a little longer, but it's not so bad. It was a decent attempt.

I lower myself to where Celia is sitting with her head between her knees. "See?" I tell Celia. "No problem. Now, all

Gemini has to do is locate the extra bone, dig it out of his skin and we're good to go."

"Oh, *gawd*," Celia groans.

She falls to her side, holding herself up with her arms. I lift her hair away from her face, thinking she's going to throw-up and maybe die like Koda said. He's right, these humanish things are fragile.

"Don't die," I tell her, shaking her shoulder.

She's breathing hard. Why is she breathing so hard?

"Please," I say. "You can't die."

Celia gulps several times. I shake her again, this time harder. "I like you, okay? I know we only just met, but I really like you."

She stills, just not in a way that makes me feel better. "You're pretty," I tell her, averting my gaze. "But you probably already know that. You're also nice and smart and good. The way you helped my friends and fought by my side, it meant a lot—" I mutter out a curse. "Just stay with me. I want you with me."

I shake her when she gasps. "Don't leave me, Celia. Not like this."

"Aric," she says through clenched teeth. "I'm not going to die. But I may puke if you keep shaking me."

I yank my hand away. "Sorry. I wasn't trying to kill you."

Celia lifts her head. "Kill me?"

"Yeah," I reply, like it's obvious. "Koda says you're fragile and that vomiting kills your kind."

"My kind?"

"Uh, huh." Folks, that's all I have.

She makes this strangling sound. I think she's getting sick, but then she starts laughing, really laughing, falling to the ground and holding her sides.

Her hair falls all over her face as she cracks up, tears rolling down her face. "Wolf," she says, trying to gather her breath between words. "I sprout fangs and claws. Trust me when I say it's going to take a lot more than puking to kill me."

She pushes up into a sitting position, her laughter dissolving when she gets a good look at Liam. "His neck is longer."

I crouch beside her. "It happens sometimes when your head gets pulled too far. His wolf grew him an extra vertebra." I take another good look. "Or three. No worries. Liam will just have to wear more turtlenecks."

Celia slowly turns to me. "That's your advice? Wear more turtlenecks?"

I don't really see the problem here, but she seems really put off by my suggestion. "His dad can break off the extra pieces when he gets home. He's better with mending than we are."

Celia starts to rise, her knees practically knocking together. "That's great, Aric. Real great. Glad to hear poor Liam won't be stuck wearing turtlenecks the rest of his life."

Celia is almost to her feet when the sound of thunder roars from the sky and lightning strikes the earth, knocking us to the ground.

From the center of the garden, a hooded figure rises, her eyes glowing and her staff pointed at my heart. "*Who dares to enter my domain?*" her angry voice booms.

I grab Celia's hand, yanking her to her feet.

Mimi has returned, and she is *pissed*.

Chapter Ten

Celia hisses low and deep, nails as sharp as daggers and as long as her hands protruding from her fingers. She's ready to fight. I'm not ready to let her. I step in front of her, blocking her with my body.

"Don't move," I warn.

More lightning. More thunder. More blood-curdling screams. "Dare you threaten me in my domain?"

Mimi has her evil hag persona firmly in place and she's not dropping it any time soon. I'm not sure what she's up to, and I'm not convinced she won't attack. I stalk forward, knowing that whatever she's up to, I'll fare better than Celia.

Mimi levitates a foot off the ground, tendrils of gray and white smoke twisting and streaming from the hem of her dress and branching toward us like tentacles. Her glowing eyes narrow at my approach. "I know you," she croaks.

She's being formal. Fair enough. I straighten to my full height, balling my hands into tight fists, letting her know I'll retaliate if provoked.

I tilt my head as a sign of respect from one powerful being to another. "I'm Aric Connor. Son of Aidan and Eliza Connor, purebred and Leader, future Alpha and protector of this young woman."

Mimi pulls back her hood. Whatever magic she used to light her eyes recedes as clumps of curly gray and white hair spill down her back. Her dark beady eyes blink back at me behind a long, crooked nose and a face that carries over a hundred years of wrinkles.

She smiles, her gray lips pulling back to reveal her crooked teeth and all the mischief she's known for. Mimi was never afraid to embrace the stereotype of a hag. I admire her for it, in a way. My issue with Mimi is that she's nuts and one hex shy of a public stoning.

"I know you," Mimi repeats, eyeing Celia without fear. "You're the one they want."

Every muscle in my frame clenches. "They can't have her."

I don't know who *they* are, but no one is hurting Celia. Not while I'm around.

Mimi descends to the ground, the tendrils beneath her dress disappearing in a cloud as her small feet hit the battered soil. She shuffles toward Celia. I growl a warning, as do Koda and Gemini, who are suddenly there, urging Celia behind them.

Mimi waves her hand dismissively, as if we're mere pests and not werewolves capable of tearing her apart.

"Hey, Aunt Mimi," Liam says.

"Liam," she says. She lifts her head, cackling when she gets a good look at his neck. "You're looking taller, boy."

Liam gives us a wink. "Told you I was her favorite."

From one blink to the next, I'm at Celia's side. Celia is small, but she's a good head above Mimi's bent frame. Celia tilts her head, something she sees in Mimi dissolving her long nails so that only her short human nails remain.

"You went hunting," Mimi tells her, any semblance of humor long forgotten. She gingerly shakes her head when Celia falls perfectly still. "If you don't learn to control your beast as you should, you will die as the dark ones intend."

"The dark ones?" I ask. My teeth grind, making it hard to speak. "Who are they, Mimi?"

Mimi's attention is lost on Celia. "So young," Mimi says. "Too young to be cursed by so much evil."

Celia's chest rises and falls in pained intakes and exhales of breath. "You made the earth to shake and signaled the bad winds to form," Mimi tells her. "The dark ones whisper your name and beg creatures bred of sin and malice to spill your blood."

The cold scent of shock fills my nose. My friends withdraw, exchanging glances. I stay put, waiting for Celia to explain, despite sensing the truth to Mimi's claims.

Celia's voice trembles. "I didn't do any of this. You have to believe me." She's no longer speaking to Mimi. She's talking to me. "Please, Aric. I didn't cause the storms or earthquakes. I don't conjure magic. The only magic I possess stays within me."

Mimi watches Celia closely. There's no fear or malice glinting in her dark eyes, but there is enough to guess Mimi understands what's happening and that we came to the right place.

"You can't wield it, girl," Mimi agrees. "But you and your sisters bathe in it." She cackles when Celia's eyes widen. "Yes, you do, precious. Yes, you do."

Mimi cackles again, this time with enough crazy to stand the hairs on the back of my neck at attention. "Celia can *change*," I begin.

"I don't speak of the tiger lurking inside of her," Mimi says. "The same beast who compels her to torture and maim."

The growl that escapes my chest is primal, my wild side begging to sink our fangs into Mimi's flesh for the insult. I'm no fool. I know Celia is capable of killing—especially if she has no choice. She has the weapons, the ability, and the strength. But torture? No. Not this sweet, pretty thing who touches me like I can break—who blushes as easily as she breathes and who won't be seen without clothes.

"Celia *wouldn't* do that," I snarl.

Mimi grins with all the crazy she's famous for. "Are you sure, young wolf, son of our most cherished Aidan and Eliza?"

Celia bows her head, glaring at the ground even as humiliation shrinks her small form inward.

I hate the way Mimi is talking to her, saying things about Celia that don't make sense. I'm ready to draw first blood and demand an apology. Except Celia isn't denying Mimi's allegations. Her lips purse tight, as terror and shame overtake her.

Terror and shame that I now know her secrets.

"Celia?" I say, my tone more wolf than man. "What did you do?"

She lifts her chin, her resolve seconds from crumbling, while her voice remains firm as stone. "I did what I had to."

She addresses Mimi, her features softening. "I may have done some of those things you claim, but I didn't cause those storms and I sure as anything didn't summon those skinwalkers."

Mimi straightens up and howls with laughter. "No. But if you wonder why they came, I can show you. Or do you prefer to remain in the dark with your pretty eyes closed?" Again, Mimi laughs, the animated and shrilled pitch scraping down my spine. "If knowledge is what you seek, come with me and I will give it."

Mimi stretches out her long, twisted fingers. I half expect a red shiny apple to form in her palm. I snag Celia's hand, no longer willing for her to have a bite of anything Mimi is offering.

Celia looks at me then back at Mimi, appearing torn.

"Come, child," Mimi says, motioning Celia toward her mess of a home. "Come and seek what you came for."

I pull Celia away from Mimi's reach. Mimi slaps my arm. "Stop it, Aric Connor. No harm will come to her by me." She turns around, shuffling toward her cave and what remains of the splintered door. "Here, kitty, kitty," she sings. "There is much to discuss, much to see, much to smoke."

"*Smoke*?" we say.

"Nice," Liam adds.

Our response earns us another cackle. Liam shrugs and strolls after Mimi. "We came for answers. Mimi wants to give them. Worst case scenario we get something to eat and we go home." He pauses and glances over his shoulder. "Or she mounts Celia's head on her wall. Either way, Mimi always has plenty of snacks."

I'm ready to break Liam's neck all over again. Koda's strong grasp on my shoulder keeps me in place, but it's Gemini's words that snag my attention. "Don't be afraid, Celia," he tells her. "I'll never let anything happen to you."

Shock drives a stake through my heart and maybe jealousy, too. I shouldn't react like this. He means well, except . . .

"We'll *all* keep her safe," Koda interjects. He drops his hand away from my shoulder. "I don't know what's going on either, Aric. And believe me, I'm less excited about being here than I was this morning. But Celia helped us. We need to help her." He motions Gemini forward. "Let's go. We'll take point in front."

"Aric," Celia says. "About what Mimi said. I . . . there's a lot more you don't know."

She's worried my opinion of her will change. "I'm not going to leave you," I promise.

She doesn't look convinced, even as we walk toward Mimi's home.

We step inside the cave behind Gemini and Koda. The only light trickles in through the mouth of the cave.

Until the battered door reforms, swallowing us in darkness.

Chapter Eleven

My eyes adjust to the darkness almost immediately. The cave is nothing more than a large open space. There's a cot in the corner and some dusty old books piled beside it to form a bedside table. An old beat-up Native American rug lies beside the bed and round, giant pillows circle a firepit made of river rocks.

Mutilated owls hang from the ceiling. There are no strings that I can see, but I do sense the power keeping them in place. I scan each one. None seem to have been hunted. It's more like they were injured or died from disease or age.

Mimi lowers herself onto a pillow and immediately a fire erupts in the pit, casting shadows along her crooked nose and deep-set eyes. Liam plops down beside her. I exchange glances with Koda and Gemini, nodding once to give them the okay to sit. Koda lowers himself next to Liam, Gemini next to Mimi. I sit beside Gemini.

It's a strategic move, leaving Celia positioned in front of Mimi with the fire between them. It's the furthest from Mimi that I can place Celia, but it doesn't seem far enough.

My attention hones on the wall behind Mimi where a human head is mounted. His brown hair is ruffled, his eyes are missing, and his skin is pulled taught against the skull.

Liam nudges Koda with his elbow and points to it. "That's my Uncle Donald. He wasn't a nice guy," he whispers, oblivious to Koda's slacking jaw.

Mimi grins, amused. She turns and lifts a large, flat wicker basket and places it just a few inches from the fire. Dry leaves, the size of platters are carefully stacked within the basket, some brown, others a deep yellow, and some so black they appear seconds from disintegrating.

The basket wasn't there before. I'm sure of it. I place my hands in front of me, cautious of what else may appear and ready to act if it has fangs.

Mimi chuckles, taking pleasure in our unease. "May I offer you some tea?" she asks.

"No. Nope. No thank you. I'm good," we say.

Except for Liam. "Got any chicken?"

"Tea and smoke, now, Liam," Mimi says. "Food when we finish."

"Sounds good, Aunt Mimi." Liam does a double-take when Koda glares at him. "What?"

Mimi smiles, fixing her attention on Celia. "What did you see at the end of the alley?" she asks. "When you had that man who reeked of sweat and whisky by the throat?" She reaches into the sleeve of her cloak and pulls out a teacup and a saucer painted with big pink roses, the edges, once rimmed with gold, chipped and cracked. Steam rises from the cup and Mimi takes a sip. "Tell me, when you felt the small bones break beneath your hold and he begged for mercy, what came to seek your soul?"

I hate how Mimi is speaking to Celia. It's not just what she says, it's how Celia reacts. She resumes that pained breathing. Anyone can see Celia didn't take pleasure in what she did, and that it came at the cost of her conscience.

"Be *nice*," I tell Mimi, my words clipped.

Mimi loses her smile, but not all the crazy. "My dear boy, this *is* me being nice."

I'm ready to leave and drag Celia with me, but the moment I reach for her hand, she shakes her head in a way that tells me she's not going anywhere.

"I don't remember much," Celia says, appearing to lose all her strength in the memory. "I was in an alley. I looked up and there was someone there."

Mimi takes another sip of tea, her motions dainty, her voice anything but. "Who?"

"I don't know," Celia answers. "She was more like a blur or an apparition. Dark. I have the feeling she was a woman, but I never saw her face. Behind her, something else appeared. She was also blurry."

"She?" Mimi asks.

"They were both females. I don't know how I know. I just do," Celia explains. "The one shrouded in white light was taller and very thin. Her hair was long and dark, past her shoulders."

"What else?" Mimi asks, when Celia stops.

Celia lowers her lashes. "That's all I remember before I woke up here."

Mimi carefully sets her tea and saucer down. It makes a *clink* when it touches the floor, but then it's gone.

"Then we must indeed smoke." She reaches for one of the giant leaves in her basket, faded yellow with a deep gold center. She twists it a few times by the stem, examining the veins closely before frowning and exchanging it for a brown one that curves into itself.

With an expert flick of her hand, Mimi tosses the large leaf into the fire. Sparks fly and the flames immediately attack the edges. I expect it to disintegrate. Instead, the leaf is slow to burn, releasing smoke in long, lazy tendrils.

Mimi closes her eyes and deeply inhales. "Ah, this shall be a good one," she says. She fans the smoke, closer to where Liam sits beside her.

Liam, because he hasn't made enough of a scene, starts laughing his ass off about the same time my legs turn to sand. Mimi cackles and everything slows down. Her laugh, our breathing, even the dead owls swinging above us.

"We have to get out here," I slur.

Koda staggers to his feet and face plants to my left.

Liam falls onto his back, snoring. Gemini crawls toward the cot and away from the door, knocking the stack of

Mimi's books over before collapsing. I'm sitting, swaying, unable to push to my feet, but somehow still upright.

"*Aric*," Celia moans.

I catch her in my arms when she tips over. "Something's wrong," she says.

I dig my heels into the dirt floor of the cave, trying to drag us away from the smoke. I fall over, still holding Celia, Mimi's cackling face fading in and out until I surrender to sleep.

My eyes blink open after what feels like a long hibernation. I'm lying on my stomach on a wooden floor beside an old bed. Toys litter the floor. A red plastic phone, colorful blocks with cartoon animals and letters, and dolls that have received plenty of love and attention. A roach skitters between a pair of discarded sneakers.

I slowly stand, careful not to make a sound. It's late, almost three in the morning, based on the wind-up clock perched on the battered bedside table. I'm in an old apartment in a bad part of town. Restless yelling from disorderly neighbors ring out from several floors above and below. Cars speed by and teens, out too late and unsupervised, scream obscenities from the streets. It's chaos outside despite the late hour, a deep contrast to the peace I sense inside this home.

In the bed, four little girls lay sleeping. The smallest one with blonde curls is tucked between two girls with jet-black hair. Celia is fast asleep at the end, closest to the door, her arms stretched out above her head, her thick lashes fanning her cheeks.

I recognize her by the way her wavy brown hair spills over her pillow and by how even in sleep, she seems on guard. She can't be more than nine, but here she is, already watching out for those she most loves.

The sound of breaking wood has me racing toward the door. My hand ghosts over the knob just as a shotgun blasts on the other side. A woman screams. The next blast silences her forever. I don't have to scent the bitter aroma of death to know as much.

The four little girls tucked beneath the sheets jolt. Celia jumps from the bed, landing in a crouch. The girl with the black curly hair lifts the baby and helps her down while the one in ponytails hunkers after Celia.

"Mama?" the baby asks.

I hold out a hand and bring a finger to my lips, trying to quiet them and keep them in place. But when the smell of blood seeps through the door and Celia's little nose twitches, I know there won't be anything I can do to hold her back.

She bolts to the door. I try to snatch her in my arms, but they go right through her and the next little girl who follows.

I charge, growling, ready to fight and ready to kill.

Four men stand over the bodies of Celia's parents, muttering in Spanish. They're not wearing masks. The sawed-off shotgun the man in front used continues to smoke. They don't care about the damage they caused, or about the four little girls frozen in terror just a few feet away. They're here to do a job and do it fast.

Celia inches forward, staring at the open chests where her parents' hearts once beat, her paling face indicative of the horror surrounding her. Blood soaks the mismatched sheets on the pullout coach where her mother and father lay, their bodies so decimated that what remains of their lifelines trickles to the edge to drip on the floor.

I leap in the air, calling forth my wolf, only to crash on the other side in human form. I leap up, swinging my arms, trying to take down the men any way I can. But my arms go through them. I'm not really here and neither is my wolf. It doesn't stop me from seeing and feeling it all.

"*Mira*," the man in a black beanie says, motioning to the girls.

He lifts the shotgun, aiming at Celia's face.

"No!"

I lurch in front of him, my arms out. He doesn't pull the trigger. He merely waits as the other men unsheathe the knives at their belts and stalk toward the little girls.

The three smallest ones are crying. Not Celia. Her tigress eyes replace her own, cementing the men in place. Her gaze latches onto each one and she deeply inhales, committing their faces and scents to memory.

Celia takes a step forward and the men take a step back, their expressions riddled with fear and shock. The man with the shotgun cocks it and aims. It's then that Celia *changes*, charging the men and sending them screaming from the apartment.

It's a small victory. The damage is done. Those men didn't wear masks for a reason. They never planned on leaving witnesses behind.

I kneel to speak to Celia, to hold her, to offer comfort for the unimaginable. But her tigress form sees past me, toward the sobbing little girls and the role of their protector she must now hold.

As the scene dissolves around me, fury and heartache churn my stomach with disgust. This is what Celia saw as a child, and what continues to haunt the beautiful girl in my arms.

I can feel her warmth and smell her delicate and sweet aroma. I hold her tighter, afraid to let go and worried what we'll see next.

This time, when I blink my eyes open, I'm sitting on an inner-city bus. Celia sits across from me, her arms crossed and her glare training on anyone who dares to look at her. Her hair is a big mane of waves, like it is in the present. She's a little younger and thinner. Her curves aren't as developed, but she remains just as fierce.

A dark green camouflage T-shirt stretches tight across her skin. Her feet are shoved into well-worn canvas sneakers and torn denim shorts that expose her lean muscular legs. It's late afternoon. Summer by the feel of the humidity thickening the air. We're back in the city her parents died in. I recognize the scent of pollution and the ripe smell of garbage.

The bus rolls to a stop and she gets off. I step off with her, wishing I could snap the necks of the men and boys leering at Celia as she bounces out. She can't see me. She can't hear me. I only wish she could.

Spanish, rap, and hip-hop music compete for attention along the stores lining the littered street. This part of the city is disgusting at best. I wrinkle my nose, overwhelmed by the scent of urine and the filth soiling the sidewalks.

"I know where you're going, and I know why you feel you have to," I say to her. "I just wish I could hunt by your side. You shouldn't be alone. Not for something like this, baby."

She's tracking the men who killed her parents. It's not just because of what she told me that I know. It's the way she carries herself and how she seems to take everything in, not willing to miss a single detail.

Anger sears my veins, melding them to my bones. If anyone *ever* hurt my parents, I would make them pay. I understand why she's here. But I can't stand that she is. As *weres,* our beasts take the brunt of our pain and torment. It's how we're able to defend and guard the earth for centuries against the evil it's exposed to.

Celia isn't a *were*. Every brush with agony she endures is hers alone to bear.

I should be with her, to protect and save her from herself. Most of all, to spare her from feeling so alone. I can taste her misery, just as I taste the salt on her skin. She's sweating and tired and too many things someone so young and kind shouldn't feel.

"*Hola, niña*," a man too old to be looking at a teenage girl calls out.

Celia whips around, the fury she pegs him with making him stumble. He crashes into another man, starting a fight. Their friends join in, turning the fight into an all-out brawl.

Celia ignores them, cutting right and down a street filled with apartments that should be condemned. This city block reminds me of purgatory. Empty souls, their life and hope long ago stolen from them, shuffle blindly along the streets, waiting for death to finish them off.

A homeless man stretches out his free hand as Celia passes. His other clutches a bottle wrapped in a paper bag. I keep pace with Celia, my keen senses taking everything in, although I'm helpless to intervene.

The next group we pass is a pimp, giving girls as young as Celia their instructions for the night. I almost lose it when he tries to snag Celia's attention, but the pimp senses she's different, respecting the predator lying beneath the surface. He's not stupid enough to follow, and just smart enough to stay alive.

With every step she takes further down the street, I struggle to stay in control. I barely manage as more of the city's damaged residents approach. Drug addicts stagger past her, scratching at their skin and begging her for money. A woman in trashy black underwear sneers at Celia, calling her names the woman likely often hears herself. Her face is swollen with bruises and track marks run up her arms. I pity her in a way. Yet, I want to pull Celia far away from her reach.

We're almost halfway down the block when Celia's determined steps slow. She stops in front of a small stoop, lifting her chin as her gaze shifts right. As I watch, her nails protrude about an inch and her nose twitches.

She found him. Her tigress showed her the way.

With a deep breath, Celia opens the door and bolts toward the stairs. I follow her up three flights. Celia's out of breath by the time she reaches the top. She's not tired. She's scared. Still, her beast drives her forward, unwilling to allow her to leave.

There are six doors on the floor. All brown and in need of sanding and a fresh coat of paint. Celia stops in front of each one, breathing deeply, taking her time. She reaches the end and starts her return, only to stop at the next door she reaches.

She presses her ear against the door and closes her eyes, listening. I close my eyes, too, breathing slowly as I extend my senses past the door and beyond.

A TV is blaring one of those old sitcoms they only show on cable. It almost muffles the soft cries of a woman. But I still hear it and so does Celia.

She pushes away from the door, glancing around.

"Don't go in there. Please," I beg. "Not by yourself."

In theory, she's supposed to live and find her way to me. Right now, that theory does nothing to ease my worry. She squeezes the doorknob and gives a hard push, breaking through the deadbolt. I respect her need for revenge. But the price she pays destroys me.

Celia walks in, trembling violently as she passes the small kitchen. The sink is overrun with dirty dishes and the floor is covered with spilled flour. Bugs skitter through the mess, greedily getting their fill. On the stove, a pot of soup with carrots and cabbage floating on top reaches a boil. Freshly made tortillas line the counter and a block of white cheese with a knife sticking from it rests on a brown plastic plate.

Someone was busy cooking. Someone else interrupted the process. Both are still here.

Celia barely glances at the kitchen or the tiny living space that follows. She stalks forward, shaking out her hands even as her claws extend.

A deep satisfied growl builds as she approaches the room where the TV's volume is set on high and the woman continues to cry. I expect her to kick open the door. I would. Instead, she slowly pokes it open with one of her nails, giving her time to take everything in, but not enough time for the man who shot her parents to act.

He watches TV with his hands folded behind his head, ignoring the young woman crying in bed beside him. She could be one of the prostitutes we saw on the way in. She could be his daughter. It doesn't matter. He doesn't care either way.

His eyes widen when he sees Celia's tigress eyes set on his throat. "*No. Por favor. No!*"

He reaches for the shotgun next to his bed. The young woman screams. But Celia is too fast for either of them. She leaps on top of him, yanking the barrel of the shotgun out of his hands and bringing the butt crashing down on his skull.

One strike. That's all it takes to splatter the contents all over the walls.

"*Dios mio!*" the woman shrieks, her Spanish accent thick. "You killed him. You killed him!"

The woman falls off the bed, trying to cover herself with the sheet, as if the flimsy fabric can somehow protect her. But this young woman isn't Celia's prey and Celia has no use for her.

Celia smashes the rifle against the wall, bending the injection port and breaking the stock. She tosses the useless thing on the floor and walks away, stopping in the kitchen long enough to swipe the tortillas in cheese.

"*Diabla*," the woman screams. "*Diabla!*"

Celia doesn't take the stairs out. She tucks the food into her shirt and charges toward the fire escape. With barely a sound, she races down the next two levels, leaping over the final railing and landing in a crouch along the narrow alleyway.

I follow, worried she's seconds from falling apart.

A few miles away, a police car blasts its sirens. Celia retraces her steps, stopping only long enough to hand the homeless man the food she stole. She hurries along, catching the next bus before it finishes closing its doors. This doesn't seem to be the right bus. It's just the one she needs to take her far away from the scene.

She drops a few bills into the slot and stretches out in the back seat. It's only when the bus moves away from the curb and onto the main road that she finally breaks down.

I can't touch her, and she can't feel me. That doesn't stop me from curling around her and wishing I could take all her pain away.

Chapter Twelve

The next few memories I experience with Celia are of her hunting the other men who killed her parents. I wake up to find her a little bit older and more troubled by her burdens.

The weather has turned cold enough to see her breath as she prowls down the street. The man she's stalking was the one who pulled his knife out first, ready to kill her and her little sisters without a second though. She follows him to a triple X movie theatre. The man sitting at the box office allows Celia through without question. I wanted to throw him through the service counter. It's clear she's underage and walking into an establishment where she doesn't belong.

Celia's only saving grace was that this mission was faster. One slash of her claws across his throat was all it took. His gurgled scream was ignored by the men sitting a few rows ahead. She shook out her hands, trying to rid herself of the blood that stained her claws.

Disgusted with the environment and by her actions, she left quickly, shoving her hands into the jacket of her coat to hide the evidence of the kill.

The next man Celia found wasn't easy prey. Not like the other two. It was very late at night. Spring had arrived, but the remaining cold was more akin to winter.

The man waited on the corner of a residential neighborhood, huddling into his coat as he spoke to someone on the phone. He pocketed his phone several minutes later, spitting at the ground and growing more impatient as time sluggishly passed by.

Celia and I watched him from the side of a boarded-up house just across the street. The grass was overgrown in most of the yards, and moonlight cast a glow along broken beer bottles carelessly tossed on the sidewalk. Despite the lack of care for the environment and that every home was in rough shape, this place was worlds better than the inner city. It still didn't make it easier to witness Celia there on her own.

A metal gate squeaked opened a few houses down and three teens swaggered out. There were three boys in gang colors and a girl on her phone trailing them. They tried to act tough, but their toughness diminished when they neared the man we'd followed.

The oldest boy nodded and passed the man a roll of wadded bills. The man exchanged the bills for what resembled a white brick secured in plastic. The boy tucked it into his pants and bunched his jacket over it. It seemed like this was his first time doing something like this. Based on his stance, it wouldn't be the last.

There were no words spoken. The deal was made and now it was done. The teens quickly dispersed, the girl continuing to talk on her phone and pretending she hadn't seen what she had, even though her strut suggested she was proud to be a part of it.

These weren't good men that Celia hunted. That didn't make the kills any easier on her.

Celia waited until the teens disappeared back into the house and the man crossed the street. She crouched low, biding her time until the man drew closer.

His close proximity should have made things easier for Celia from a hunter's perspective, except this man was used to fighting those bigger and stronger than him.

Celia pounced, snagging him in a headlock and covering his mouth so he couldn't scream. Rage blazed across his eyes as Celia dragged him behind the house. He kicked her in the knee, hard enough to cause her to lose her hold. She limped after him, tackling his waist and bringing him down on the sidewalk.

They rolled around, each fighting for control. The thin jacket Celia wore offered little protection against the broken glass. It cut into the fabric, puncturing her skin and allowing blood to seep through.

The man kicked at her, striking her hard in the nose and momentarily stunning her. He staggered into the next yard, securing a large stick and breaking it across Celia's jaw when she charged. Her mouth pooled with blood, but this time, she wasn't letting go.

Celia clung to him, grabbing tight to his head as he begged for mercy. If he could have heard me, I would have told him Celia had no mercy left to give. She snapped his neck, the blood spilling from her mouth soaking his coat when she finally let him go.

Celia hobbled onto the bus several blocks later. She dropped her money, keeping her scarf pressed tightly against her face. Most of the passengers ignored her. Some stared. But not one person asked if she was okay.

"She's a kid!" I yelled to them. "She's hurt and alone. What's wrong with you people?"

My shouts meant nothing to them or to her. Again, I fell to her side, offering her gentle words she couldn't hear and an embrace I never wanted to break.

"One more, baby," I said to her. "Just one more."

The best way I could describe the moments that followed were that I fell into a state of mourning. Celia hadn't died, but her innocence and spirit had taken a harsh beating.

I cursed several times. The beast controlled Celia and incited her need to hunt. She didn't understand that this desire for vengeance scared Celia, and failed to offer the retribution her tigress felt she deserved. The way Celia trembled and how she curled into herself afterward was hard to watch. Yet, I couldn't help thinking the actions of her beast were righteous.

As terrified and hurt as Celia was, she needed to do this for her and her sisters.

And she couldn't do it without the help of her tigress.

My reasoning did little to comfort me. Like I said, my beast could protect my conscience and ease the strain my actions caused. Celia's tigress didn't have that same power.

"I want to keep you with me," I whispered, my lips grazing over her cheek. "I can't let you go back to that life."

I meant what I said, but she didn't hear a word of it.

Like the times before, I watched her cry. There was one more to hunt. I only hoped this one would give us some answers.

Chapter Thirteen

The darkness encasing me dimly shifts into light, forcing my eyes open even though my feet were walking long before I could see.

I'm shadowing Celia. The weather is as hot and humid as it was when we first started hunting and Celia is more like I remember her now. A black tank top stretches across her back, the hem long enough to brush the rear pockets of her tight jeans.

The man we're following is drunk, the bottle of whisky he's carrying swinging back and forth as he sings. It's a ballad of lost love. It's as much as I make out with the little Spanish I know.

I glance over my shoulder, feeling like we're being followed. "Celia," I say, catching up to her. "I think she's here."

She, meaning the witch. I can feel her magic and power. It's strong, like the scent of the jungle following a storm, odd considering where we are. I frown, sensing something immature about it, as if she hasn't quite figured out how to manipulate the gamut of power she's carrying. A young witch perhaps? Or someone naïve and not yet skilled with magic?

Celia keeps her focus ahead, ignoring the catcalls of the boys pretending to be men, who loiter on the next corner we pass. It's yet another moment I wish I was actually present. They wouldn't dare disrespect her if I was here.

My head whips in the opposite direction when I feel another wave of magic stir nearby. This one is stronger, darker, with enough menace to make me growl. We keep walking, our steps faster when the man we're following tries to climb into a car.

The door swings open and two women scramble out, screaming at him as they shove him away and slap at his face. The man laughs, having fun at their expense. He staggers away, almost losing his footing as he continues his song. Another growl rumbles my chest when I feel yet another dark form appear, and another after that.

There are three witches, plus the one I first sensed. The first feels threatened by the others. She doesn't seem to think she can take them. She skitters away, frightened, the scent of the wild jungle disappearing with her.

That young witch is terrified for a reason. We shouldn't be here. Not alone.

"Celia!" I yell. "Celia! We have to get out of here. There are three dark witches following you. Not just one."

I turn, walking backwards. Less than a block away, I feel the presence of darkness, then again to my far right and once more toward the left. The witches have spotted Celia and they're closing in, fast.

Celia is no longer the hunter. She's become the prey.

The man turns around, sensing he's being followed. I don't expect him to recognize Celia, not when her eyes remain human. Somehow, he does.

"*La diabla*," he screams. "*La diabla*."

He calls Celia the she-devil, just as the woman who witnessed Celia's first kill did. Of course. With his other buddies dead, he must have guessed he'd be next. And by the looks of it, so did the witches trailing us. But how?

The man throws his bottle at Celia and charges into traffic. She easily ducks out of the way, but not as easily around the cars speeding forward. An old Chevy almost mows her over. But as fast as this truck is going, Celia's reflexes are easily two steps ahead. She rolls over the hood instead of leaping over it, hitting the ground running as she swerves around the remaining cars.

Celia curses when she reaches the walkway and sees the man race into a crowded parking deck. She starts forward without me. I only hesitate, because I know we're not alone.

The dark witches separate like hyenas ready to take down their kill. They're not nearly as fast, but Celia is on her own and unaware of their presence.

Celia stops at the entrance to the garage. The way she listens makes me think she picked up on the witches until she cuts through the garage and out the other side. The man lured her into the deck to confuse her, but his drunken state made him sloppy and loud. She hears him exit and thinks she has him.

We give chase, running across another busy street. While I know I technically can't get hit, I don't take any chances, not with the dark forces I feel behind us.

I let out a breath when I see him near an alley. This is it. The place Celia gets cornered.

Celia surges forward, snagging the man by the collar and throwing him into the alley.

"No . . . *por favor*," the man begs. "Don't kill me, little one."

Celia ignores him, her attention shifting right and left before storming forward.

"No," the man says again. "Please. I have children."

Celia hoists him up by the throat. "No. You don't. But my parents did."

I hear the crunch of bones, but I don't look. All at once, dark magic penetrates the end of the alley. Of the three witches who followed, the strongest has come for Celia and the others aren't far away.

I growl, guarding Celia with my body. "Stay away from her," I warn, already sensing the pain the witch wants to inflict. She's not just here to kill Celia. She's here to make her scream.

The witch raises her staff, the amount of energy she casts into her spell damaging the veil she used to camouflage herself.

Celia turns, finally sensing the magic the witch kept carefully hidden.

It's then the other witch, the young one who reminded me of the jungle and whose power is not fully realized, appears.

The dark witch didn't see me, but the younger witch meets me dead in the eyes.

"*Salvarla*!" she screams, filling the alley with white light.

I startle awake in Mimi's cave with Celia shaking uncontrollably in my arms. My friends surround us, their expressions tight with worry.

Mimi watches Celia closely, brushing her hair away from her head in a gentle manner I don't expect. "You have to get up, little tigress," she says. "They're coming for you."

Koda rushes to the door, peering out through the small peephole as I help Celia to her feet. "There's nothing there."

Mimi shuffles to the now dwindling fire. "But there will be, and it's too late to run," she says. "Liam. Be a dear and have some of this bird, won't you, precious? I don't want it to go to waste."

Mimi turns, hoisting a silver platter of fried breast meat and legs that wasn't there before.

"Sure, Aunt Mimi. Thanks," he says. He lifts the platter from her hands. "Hey, you guys want some?"

Koda is ready to slap Liam upside the head and he's not alone. "Are you seriously going to eat right now?"

Liam frowns. "You heard Mimi. It'll go to waste if I don't."

"Good boy." Mimi pats his arm, returning her attention to the fire.

"*Good boy*?" Koda hollers. "Liam, you didn't see what Aric and I saw—"

"Wait," Gemini interrupts. "You were there, too? When Celia fought the man who bloodied her face?"

My head jerks in his direction.

"Someone bloodied her face?" Koda growls. Gemini nods. "No. That's not what I saw. Aric and Celia were in an apartment. One of the men who killed her parents was there, in bed with a young woman—"

"My parents," Celia stammers. "You saw what happened to them?"

Koda's skin grows an odd shade of gray. "Yeah. I saw." He turns back in the direction of the door, unable to meet Celia's bruised expression.

"Gemini," I say. "What did you see?"

Gemini's expression steels. "I saw the night Celia lost her parents. Then I saw you and Celia hiding behind an abandoned house. I wasn't physically there. It was more like watching a movie."

"Speaking of movies," Liam says between chews. "I saw you walk into that theatre." His expression turns stony. "After what he did to your folks, he deserved what he got and more."

Koda and Gemini tilt their heads in agreement. They mean well, but there's no disguising Celia's shame.

Perspiration gathers along her crown. She lifts her chin from where she's pressed against my chest. "You were there?" she asks. "With me?"

"I never left you," I tell her.

"How could you?" Mimi scoffs. "Your wolf has latched onto her tigress."

"What?" I ask, my attention bouncing between Celia and Mimi. "*Why?*"

Mimi cackles, her concentration on the firepit never faltering. "Why do you think?"

I don't move. No. She can't mean . . .

"I'm sorry," Celia says, her trembling alternating between severe and less pronounced. "I never wanted you to see what I've been through." She bows her head. "Or what I've done."

I stroke her cheek, wishing I could take away the memories that haunt her. "I'm sorry, too. Not because of what you did, but what it did to you."

Thunder rolls in the distance. It's different than the thunder that accompanied Mimi's arrival, more like a screech of madness than anything nature could summon.

"Koda," I say, sensing a freakish change in the atmosphere. "What's out there?"

Koda doesn't appear to pick up on what I'm feeling. But he does infer that something's wrong. "Nothing," he replies, peering outside. "I say we make a run for it while the coast is clear."

He wrenches the door open, only for it to slam shut before he can clear it. He grabs the knob, pulling it hard, but it won't give.

I turn to Mimi. "Why are you keeping us here?" I demand.

Mimi pulls another steaming cup of tea from her sleeve, her attention on the crackling embers alternating in shades of gold and red. "I told you, it's too late to run. They'll come for the tigress and anyone with her."

"I'll go alone." Celia steps from my reach. "I'm fast. I can lead them away from you—"

"*No*," I snarl. "That's not an option."

Koda positions himself to my right. "We're not leaving you, Celia. We're in this together."

Liam, now done with his snack, edges closer, cracking his knuckles. "We didn't get to help you track down those men, but we can help you now."

"Wait a moment," Gemini says. He looks to Mimi. "We came here for answers and we have none. Why did we see what we did?"

Mimi sips on her tea as another screech of thunder bellows. This one a lot closer. "That's a good question," she replies.

"*You mean you don't know?*" Koda growls at her.

I don't blame Koda for his harsh response. It's taking everything I have to keep from lashing out. "What *do* you know?" I snap.

"Celia is cursed by darkness, as are her sisters," Mimi answers simply. But as she continues to speak, it seems her words are only meant for Celia. "The curse backfired, my dear. Something meant to kill gave you the tigress, the wielder of fire and light, the mistress of weaponry, and the healer, instead."

"Your other sisters' powers," I guess.

Celia didn't mention what her other sisters can do, protecting them as she's always done, even from me.

Mimi places her teacup on the saucer, appearing to work through her thoughts. "The lighter power knew you were in trouble and that they were coming for you."

"They?" I ask. My narrowing gaze tightens. "And who are they, exactly?"

"You're asking me, young wolf?" Mimi asks. "You sensed them, all of them. What can you tell me of their power?"

"What is she talking about?" Koda asks.

"I was with Celia when she chased down the last of her prey—"

"Don't," Celia says, scrunching her eyes closed. "Please don't refer to them that way."

It's what they were, but Celia can't seem to wrap her mind around it. How can she, when there's such a disconnect between her and her beast?

"Three dark witches followed us," I say, carefully choosing my words. "I'm sure that's what they were. But there was another one, a light one, who was young and awkward." It's a strange word to use, but thinking back, it's the only one that fits.

"Awkward?" Gemini repeats, glancing toward Koda. "What do you mean?"

"Her power was different from the others. It was strong, but raw and uncontrolled. The dark witches didn't have that problem. They were well-trained and organized."

Koda frowns. "Just so I'm clear, this light witch was out-matched, but she still went after the dark ones?"

"Not exactly," I say. "I think she knew she couldn't take them in a fight. That didn't stop her from trying to help Celia. The dark one, though . . ." I shudder, remembering the feel of her kind of evil. "The dark one was too much for both of them.

"Both meaning the light witch and Celia?" Gemini asks.

It's hard for those who have inner beasts not to feel superior to all other supernaturals. Gemini has seen first-hand how tough and smart Celia is. But what I felt was deadly and beyond Celia's abilities.

Celia doesn't possess what it takes to make a kill, make it count, and walk away without it affecting her. The dark witch who shadowed us was all about death and suffering, taking pleasure in the malice she inflicts.

"Neither stood a chance," I confess.

I don't like admitting what I do, especially to Celia. "I'm not certain what happened to the other two dark witches. I think they were close, but only the strongest presented herself," I explain. "As Celia mentioned before, this dark figure appeared at the end of the alley. But then the light materialized immediately behind her."

Mimi agrees. She didn't mention taking that journey with us, but whatever she saw was enough. "The light couldn't vanquish the dark," she says. "Not this time. So, she sent Celia where she would be safe." She shakes her head. "But it cost the light dearly. She paid the ultimate price for interfering with those who seek to kill Celia."

"She's dead," Celia guesses. "The person who helped me?"

Mimi tucks her tea and saucer back into the sleeve of her cloak. "Nothing can help her now."

We all quiet. If not for another closer screech of thunder I think more time would have passed in silence. "Why did the light witch send me here?" Celia asks. "Until now, I didn't know anyone in Colorado."

Mimi smiles. "Did you not hear her words, child? *Salvala*. 'Save her,' she said." She turns from Celia and looks me dead in the eyes. "The light sent you to the safest place you could be."

"Colorado?" Liam asks, confused.

"No," Mimi replies, her voice lowering. "*With Aric*."

Celia and I look at each other. I think I should say something, but something isn't coming.

"I need to get back to my sisters," Celia says.

"No," Mimi says. "If you survive what's coming, you'll only lead the dark ones to those you love." Mimi puckers her wrinkled brow. "Oh. Looks like the dark ones are already here."

She shuffles to the door and opens it. A torrent of power detonates above us and thousands of mini-lightning bolts blast into the soil, rocking the earth and knocking everyone over.

Mimi brushes herself off as she rises. "Humpf," she says. "This is worse than I thought."

If Mimi is trying to piss me off, it's working.

We scramble to our feet, stopping in front of the door. From each pocket of broken soil, something stirs. Lots of little somethings. A small pointy spike, covered in armor, pokes through the ground. It swings back and forth, feeling its surroundings before scurrying out.

"Okay. Scorpions," Liam says. "That's not so bad. Hey, they're kind of cute."

The scorpion is tiny. Just a baby. It shakes off the dirt covering it, each shift causing him to grow and his body to expand. Beside it, another scorpion emerges, only for the first scorpion to sting it with its now much longer tail.

The smaller scorpion flips upside down, *screaming*, its legs thrashing wildly and the pinchers making a high-pitched clicking sound. As we watch with our jaws on the ground, it turns a sickly gray and begins to decompose, splitting open and exposing its sticky innards.

The bigger scorpion devours it piece by piece, each swallow doubling its size, until he reaches the diameter of a full-grown tortoise.

"Well," Mimi says. "That's disturbing."

And then she giggles.

More scorpions appear, growing in size and devouring those too slow to grow or get out of the way. "All right," Liam concedes. "We might have a small problem."

At the sound of Liam's voice, one of the larger scorpions throws itself at the opening to the cave. It bangs against Mimi's invisible ward. The scorpion shrieks, the power of Mimi's magic sizzling through its armor.

An army of smaller scorpions don't waste time, crawling over their brethren and eating him alive.

I drag my hand across my face. "The wards are holding, but we can't stay here forever."

"Nonsense," Mimi says. She shuffles back in the direction of the firepit. "My wards won't hold longer than a few minutes."

"*What*?" the rest of us ask.

Another scorpion throws itself at the ward, causing it to sparkle and split down the side.

Mimi steps into the fire, her right foot disappearing as she does so.

"Where the hell do you think you're going?" Koda bellows.

"I'm not staying here," Mimi tells him. She points to herself. "I want to live."

"So, do we!" Koda fires back.

Mimi bats her hand, sinking into the firepit. "I need time to figure out Celia's predicament." She frowns when I glare at her. "That's what you sought me for, was it not?"

"That's before we knew what was coming," I snarl.

Mimi cackles. "You have me there, wolf."

Her crow-like laughter echoes around us as she dissolves into the sizzling embers. "She left us," Koda says. "That nutcase up and left us."

A third scorpion slams against the ward. This one breaks through. I skewer it with a fire poker before it can cause any damage and toss it into the flames. Unlike Mimi, it doesn't disappear. It screams and twitches, its insides sizzling as it pops open. The smell is acidic and sharp, making us cough.

More scorpions gather close to the door, testing out the ward with their pointy tails and searching for weak points. The ward barely sparks. Mimi's protection spell is all but gone.

"All right. Okay," I say, willing myself to form a plan. "We're going to have to fight our way out." I hand Celia the poker. "You're not immune to scorpion venom, are you?" She shakes her head. "Don't worry. We are. Stay between us and don't give these things a chance to sting you."

"Aric," Gemini says. "These scorpions are bred from dark magic. Our wolves may be able to fight off the first few shots of venom, but the more we are injected with, the longer it will take to clear our systems. With enough stings, we'll be rendered useless, giving them time to eat us."

"Guys?" Liam says.

"We're not going to be eaten," I bite out. "No way are we going down like this!"

"Guys?" Liam repeats, this time moaning. His hand is pressed against the wall of the cave. By the looks of his paling face, it's the only thing keeping him up.

Another scorpion breaks through. Koda immediately kicks it, smashing its protective exterior against the stone wall.

Celia grasps Liam's arm when he starts to fall. His stomach is pushing in and out in odd, mutated motions. "What's wrong with him?" she asks.

Liam foams at the mouth, barely able to speak. "I think there was something wrong with the chicken Mimi gave me."

We jump as Mimi's cackle reverberates from everywhere in the cave. "I never said it was chicken."

Her cackles fade as Liam worsens. He falls on all fours, spitting out what resembles wet cotton.

"What is that?" Koda asks.

Celia looks up from where she's kneeling beside Liam. "I think it's plumage."

"*What*?" Koda yells.

Mimi has really outdone herself this time. "Mimi hit Liam with a spell," I manage.

Koda stamps another two scorpions that break through as Liam throws up a round spotted ball. It rolls forward, stopping at my feet.

"Is that an *egg*?" Gemini asks.

"I think so," Liam says. He eases to his feet with Celia's help, wiping his mouth with the back of his hand.

"This whole thing is *messed up*," Koda says.

I can't argue. I don't know where Mimi is headed with this. I'm only hoping it's somewhere semi-sane.

The egg cracks open and a baby owl spills out. It chirps, looking at Celia. It chirps again.

"I think it's hungry," Liam says. "Hey, Celia. Are you up to breastfeeding?"

"It has *a beak*, Liam," Celia reminds him.

"Is that a no?" Liam asks.

About seven scorpions spill through the crack in the ward. Koda kills the first two. Gemini and I go after the other ones. Celia slams the poker into a scorpion that escapes our wrath, making it scream as its guts spurt out.

The little owl scoots toward Celia, stopping in front of the mutilated scorpion. It starts to feed on it, causing its feathers to sprout and its body to grow. A few bites. That's all it takes for the little owl to triple in size.

By the time it finishes growing, the owl is almost as tall as my hip and we've squashed at least three dozen more scorpions.

Koda curses as he looks out across Mimi's property. "There're still hundreds out there!"

The owl hoots, glancing up at the dead owls lining the ceiling. Celia and Liam jump when one that's missing an eye blinks at them with two very new, very bright eyes. It flutters its feathers, flapping its wings several times before leaving its perch to devour another dead scorpion.

Another hoot follows a rise of magic that screams of Mimi.

"Gemini?" I say, watching the last few owls come to life.

Gemini steps out of the way of the swooping birds, watching them eagerly feast on the scorpions. "Yes?" he asks.

"Owls hunt and kill scorpions, don't they?"

I don't have to look at him to know he's smiling. I'm too busy taking in how fast the owls are growing. "Scorpions are part of their diet," Gemini agrees.

Mimi is in dire need of a straightjacket and she's borderline psychotic and unpleasant most of the time.

But that hag can wield a spell.

Chapter Fourteen

The owls lead the charge, swooping out of the cave behind the one Liam birthed, its fervent hoots urging them on. The wolves and I follow, beating into the scuttling scorpions with our feet and bare hands.

The owls were dead until moments ago. As Mimi's spell fades, they'll likely return to their posts. Until then, they're living and soaring and *eating*, flapping their immense wings and tearing into the scorpions.

The leader dives down, snagging one of the larger scorpions in its talons. Another jets toward it, snagging a claw. Together, they rip it in half, the remains of the scorpion sending the other owls into a frenzy and enticing them to attack.

"Look out!" Celia screams.

I think she's yelling to Liam, until the original scorpion, now longer and meaner, whips its tail right at my heart.

The stinger grazes my skin, but it doesn't penetrate. I dodge out of its reach when it strikes again, only for it to turn on Celia when it sees her exposed.

Celia swings the poker and clips the tail. The scorpion shakes off the dead stump, growing another stinger in the time it takes before he leaps again. The creature's movement are quick and exact. Celia takes another swing, aiming low. She barely nicks it and doesn't come close to hurting it.

She leaps backward, the wicked thing slicing at the fabric of her dress and almost stinging her. I break open the two other scorpions I'm fighting like lobsters and go after the one bent on killing Celia.

I don't wait for it to strike again. I snatch it by the tail and pound its body into the ground like a hammer. Over and over it collides against the earth until the tail rips off and the lower half stops moving.

"Aric!" Celia yells.

She's edging back toward the cave. Liam is near the garden. Gemini and Koda are on the path leading back to the forest.

The scorpions have separated us. We're several yards away from each other. But it ends now.

The first thing I learned as a wolf was to *never* separate from your pack. You hunt and you bring down your enemy as one.

"Regroup, now!" I yell.

I charge toward Celia, kicking the scorpions in my path onto any hard object I find, or up into the air and toward the ravenous owls. Mimi doesn't have much we can use as a weapon out here, but I have plenty of anger.

I send one giant scorpion soaring across the yard, slamming it into another around the same size. They attack one another, striking their stingers like cobras and forgetting all about us.

I ignore them, dashing toward Celia as she climbs on top of Mimi's cave to avoid the band of scorpions scuttling after her. "Celia!"

Every part of me stalls as Celia leaps backward off the top of the cave, doing some flippy thing and landing full force on two super-sized scorpions. She doesn't stop there. She kicks the remains of one scorpion into several smaller ones that leap toward her, stunning them and allowing the owls to attack. She then brings down the poker onto the head of another.

Never has a woman been this *hot*.

The entire incident happens in mere seconds. If I wasn't a *were,* I would have missed most of it. Celia sprints toward me, kicking away the smaller scorpions flicking their tails at her.

I blindly catch a leaping scorpion and break it in two, tossing it aside as Celia reaches me, barely aware that I'm gawking.

Celia jumps, using her weight to crush those she can't beat to death with the poker. I snatch two more that jump, feeling their hard shells snap beneath my grip, but not before their claws rip at my flesh.

Like Gemini said, these aren't regular scorpions. One manages to sting my calf before I can stomp on it, its venom burning my flesh like liquid fire.

The invasion into my system awakens the healing components of my wolf. It attacks the venom, localizing it before it can spread and destroying what's left of it. Another few stings and I'll be on the ground. But hell will freeze over before I let anything hurt Celia or my friends.

I snatch another one that leaps toward Liam's exposed neck as he reaches us, mutilating it with my hands before it can sting.

Koda joins us, followed by Gemini.

"More than half are down," I yell, over the excited tittering of the owls. "Let's get this done and get out!"

There's no grace to our movements, no organization, no precision strikes or mad skills that make us look sleek. You won't find Superman among us. No. The Hulks are in the house and hulks *smash*.

These scorpions jump high. When they do, our fists sail, punching as we would any opponent stupid enough to cross us. When they don't leap, our feet find them, stomping hard enough to kill or stun them. These aren't just bugs, scampering around and trying to hide. They come at us full force, like hungry locusts invading a large field.

Nothing we practiced ever prepared us for an attack like this. That doesn't mean we're not crippling these things, or that the owls Mimi sent aren't effective.

I'm not sure how long it takes. An hour, maybe longer. Koda makes the final kill, his large foot coming down on the last of the scorpions. I tried to avoid the stingers and I think I would have avoided most of them if I hadn't been trying so hard to spare Celia.

She falls into a crouch, covering her mouth when she sees the large hole burrowing through my right thigh. The final few kills cost me. But Celia is safe and that's all that matters.

"Don't touch it," I say, when she reaches out her hand. "My wolf is already mending it."

Her large, soulful eyes blink back at me. "Does it hurt?" she asks.

"Totally," Liam interrupts. He turns around, exposing his back. Gray lines branch out, spreading the venom and leaving indentations of melting skin. As the venom reaches his shoulders, the power of his wolf pushes it back, centralizes it and smoothing the damaged tissue.

It doesn't take long for Liam's wolf to repair him from the inside out. It also doesn't take much longer for him to speak. "I tried to get creative and trample them with my back." He makes a face. "It wasn't a good idea."

Celia rises. "Liam, I'm so sorry."

"Don't worry about him," Koda says. "He'll be all right."

Celia gasps when she sees the chunk of arm Koda's wolf is working overtime to fill in. "Koda," she says. "You poor thing."

Very gently, Celia takes Koda's wrist, turning it back and forth so she can examine the extent of the damage. Koda's face turns two shades redder than Mimi's squashed tomatoes. "Uh. It's fine," he says, tripping over his words.

"It looks awful." Her words cut off when Koda shrinks away. "Why is your face so red?" She reaches up on her toes to feel his head. "Is the venom making you feverish?"

Liam cracks up. "No *way*. Koda is blushing. Gemini, are you seeing this? Celia is totally making Koda blush."

Which makes Celia blush, Koda's face reddens further, and oh, boy, isn't *this* fun?

"I'm sorry," Celia says. "I wasn't trying to embarrass you."

"It's okay," Koda says, his flaming face turning up another notch. "I just, you know what I mean."

"Nah, we don't," Liam says, grinning ear to ear. "Please, elaborate and enlighten our feeble, yet studly, minds."

"Liam," Gemini interrupts. "Now is not the time."

He starts walking, but neither of my knucklehead friends follow. They're too busy waiting on Celia, who seems unable to detach herself from Koda. As if on cue, the wind lifts their hair, making them look like they should be on the cover of some sappy young adult novel. Awesome.

"You don't owe me an explanation," Celia tells him. In general, her voice sounds a little gruff, reflecting the worst of the world she's seen. It shouldn't come across as gentle as it does. Somehow, she manages just fine. "I just want to make sure you're all right. All of you are hurt only because you tried to help me."

"Females tend to stay away from me," Koda blurts out. "I've never had one touch me."

I think Koda was trying to make Celia feel better. Instead, he ended up revealing an ugly truth about his life.

Females are drawn to me, because of my status. They seek Liam out, gushing about how "cute" he is. Gemini is considered handsome, although his quieter disposition keeps those who might be interested in him at a distance. Then there's Koda.

A few girls I've met have seen Koda's picture on my phone. Most of them jabber on about how "hot" he is. One went as far as to call him the future father of her children. But then they meet him and everything his wolf does to harden and protect him against the cruelty he's endured rises to the surface, causing those interested females to look elsewhere.

Koda shuffles after Gemini, embarrassed for admitting what he does.

"Why?" Celia asks.

Koda pauses, scowling over his shoulder. He thinks she's placating him, but then he sniffs and realizes she's genuinely confused. His frown dissolves. "I guess they're intimidated."

"I know how you feel." Celia shrugs. "Males tend to stay away from me—"

"Naw. *Really*? I don't believe it," my friends interrupt.

Great, now it's time for Celia to blush. It's taking everything I have not to nail my pals with chunks of dead scorpion.

Celia covers her face, trying to get it together. She drops her hand away, speaking fast. "My sisters would be more than happy to hang out with you. Especially Shayna."

Koda perks up. "Yeah?"

Celia smirks. "Koda, she would talk your ear off."

With all the attention she's getting, I'm sure Celia forgot all about me. But then she turns to me, smiling in that way she only seems to do around me. "Are you ready, wolf?"

"Yeah, let's go." I start forward, limping. Next to Celia, Gemini suffered the least amount of damage. I might have suffered the worst. The hole in my thigh burrowed into the bone, making it harder for my wolf to heal it quickly. I can't stretch out my leg yet, but the venom is mostly gone, and the wound has begun to knit closed.

Celia jogs to my side. "Here. Let me carry you."

I jump away when she bends and opens her arms. "What are you doing?"

"It's okay," she assures me. "I'm a lot stronger than I look."

"If my bloody corpse lay covered in scorpions as my decapitated head looked on, I still wouldn't let you carry me."

She crosses her arms, one eyebrow raised. "If you were decapitated, you wouldn't be able to see anything, let alone protest."

My friends crack up, even Gemini, who's trying to hide it by wiping his mouth.

"Ow, Celia," Liam whines. "I think the scorpions hurt my little toe and Koda's pinky. Could you carry me? Maybe both of us? We promise to let you."

"Knock it off," I growl, hoping Celia doesn't take them up on it.

"I'm sure you big, menacing wolves will be fine on your own," Celia says, glancing down.

Her cheeks are still pink when she looks up at me, strands of her hair partially covering the left side of her face. "Will you walk with me?"

I clear my throat, dropping my voice several octaves. "Someone has to keep you safe," I growl.

With my head held high and my leg almost healed, I march forward, allowing my friends to lead the way. In my periphery, I catch Celia's fingers lift toward mine. The movement is subtle, and I almost don't see it. I think she's trying to hold my hand, but then thinks better of it.

My head lowers as I thread her fingers through mine. I've never considered myself the shy type. In the past, I'd shake my head when Gem withdrew from females or when Koda intimidated them simply by being. I didn't understand why it was so hard for them to connect with the opposite sex.

Then came Celia.

Being this shy and insecure around a female doesn't seem fitting, especially after years of being told what a catch I am. But if I'm going to feel this way, I can't think of anyone else I'd rather feel it with.

The warmth that spreads between us when our skin touches is like sunshine following a long week of storms. She makes everything worth it, all the good and all the bad.

"Thank you for the Wonder Woman underwear," she whispers. She nibbles on her bottom lip. "They're a little small, but she's my favorite."

And you're mine, I almost tell her. I'm realizing that more and more, unsure how I've gone my whole life without knowing her.

The owls sweep down from the sky, settling on any perch they can find to watch us leave.

"What if there are more scorpions?" Celia asks, glancing behind her.

I motion to the owls. "They'll take care of them."

The earth shifts around us as the destruction in Mimi's yard begins to repair itself. Stalks bearing fruit too large for their vines straighten, spilling over the garden gates attempting to seal them in.

There's power and then there's Mimi.

We reach Gemini's wolf, the remains of several scorpions littering the ground around him. The elk we brought is gone. Mimi took her payment.

We start out in a jog back to my place. Behind us, the owls take to the sky, circling the area as Mimi's cackles erupt.

"You're staying with me again tonight," I tell Celia, giving her hand a light squeeze.

"Are you sure?" Celia says. "You heard Mimi, anyone who's with me is in danger."

"Then we'll be in danger together," I say, reassuring her that she's not in this mess alone.

"What's wrong?" I ask when she stares blankly ahead.

"Mimi said my sisters will be in danger if I go back."

I stiffen, recognizing how scared she must be. "That's right."

"Does this mean I can't go back? Ever?"

"No," I say. I'm not trying to make promises I can't keep. Somehow, I'll find a way to help her. "It just means we have to figure out another way."

It's like her heart breaks right in front of me. "And if we can't?" she asks.

Then stay with me and be my family so I'll never have to know a day without you.

"We will," I promise.

I don't tell her what I'm thinking. I can't. Not when the thought of losing her hurts as much as it does.

Chapter Fifteen

The run over the mountain and back to my place is quicker than our initial run to Mimi's. Then again, we didn't worry about an attack from supernatural insectoids on our way there.

What a day. We're tired and hungry. As *weres*, our supernatural bodies will eventually develop so we can fight for days without stopping. For now, our bodies are still growing and the need for rest is as important as our next meal.

Celia keeps up. I'm not sure how. Although she was spared from the scorpion venom, the exertion and the bumps and bruises she acquired must have done a number on her. I'm starting to learn that unable to heal or not, it's going to take a lot to bring this little kitty down.

Gemini's twin wolf runs alongside Celia, panting and looking up at her while leaping and avoiding the hazards of the mountain terrain, as if no obstacle matters as much as her. Totally love-struck, his tongue dangles from the side of his mouth and his tail wags as he runs. My wolf isn't doing anything close to tail wagging. Mostly, he's raring to take a bite out of Gemini.

Celia laughs when the goofball leaps up and butts her elbow. She pets his head. "Looking for a little attention there, buddy?" she asks.

My glare cuts to Gemini. "Yeah, a little lonely there, *buddy*?"

Gemini grins, his face reddening when Koda and Liam throw their heads back in laughter.

"What's wrong, Aric?" Koda says. "A little jealous there, pal?"

"Naw," Liam says. "Not our fearless Leader, Aric. He'd have to like Celia to feel threatened." He cuts in front of me, running backwards and trying to throw my pace off. "Do you like, Celia, Aric? Do you think she's pretty? Do you dream that one day you'll make pups together—"

"Liam, look out." He whips around. I trip him before he realizes nothing is there. He crashes to the ground, kicking up dirt.

And suddenly, all is right with the world.

Celia gasps. "You tripped him."

"No." I grin, lying through my teeth. "That was a total accident."

"So is this," Gemini says. His twin zips in front of me. I leap over him. I don't quite plant my feet as the incline drops when Gemini tackles me to the ground. We topple down the mountain, both trying to get the upper hand.

We crash into a muddy creek with Gemini's twin wolf circling and yipping. I drag and lift Gemini into a full Nelson, using his body as a shield to keep his twin from leaping on top of me. Koda is roaring with laughter. Liam reaches us then, lifting a pile of mud in his hand. I guess what he's going to do and duck.

Liam nails Koda in his opened mouth with a good chunk of mud. "Oops," Liam says, laughing. "Sorry."

Koda is spitting and drooling mud. "What the fluk, Liam?" he growls, which only makes the rest of us laugh harder.

Koda crashes into Liam, their large bodies colliding into us as we continue to fight for the upper hand. We roll to a stop against a tree, freezing when we see Celia sitting quietly on a small boulder. She smiles when she sees us, but I notice how tired she seems and I'm not alone.

Gemini's twin trots over to her, releasing a small whine. "She needs food," Gemini says.

I'm already on my feet. "Yeah. Let's get back."

Koda has Liam in a choke hold, trying to feed Liam mud. Liam's extra-long neck makes it hard for Koda to secure his grip and Liam is doing his best to bite him. Gemini jogs over to separate them. I immediately go to Celia.

"Hey," I say. "Are you all right?"

She nods and offers a small smile. "I'm fine if I keep going, but if I stop . . ." She shrugs. "I'm just a little tired is all."

I open my mouth, but she cuts me off by lifting her hand. "Before you ask, no, you may not carry me."

"I wasn't going to offer," I say.

"Liar," she says.

"Yup," I agree, unable to stop my smirk.

We take off again, my friends yapping it up and apologizing for their actions. Me, I mostly keep quiet, watching Celia to make sure she's okay. She starts off slow and at first, I worry that the brief rest did more harm than good. But like the trooper she is, Celia resumes her quick pace.

"Sorry about the fight back there," I say when I see her color improve. "*Weres* roughhouse all the time. We're no exception and I'm pretty sure we engage in it more than others."

"It's all right," Celia says. "It's been a stressful day and you boys look like you needed to release some energy."

"I take it you and your sisters don't wrestle in mud?"

Celia laughs. "No. Taran and I occasionally go at it—"

"Naked?" Liam asks, a little too enthusiastically.

I don't know which is worse, what he asks or how my friends light up and wait for her to respond.

Celia rolls her eyes. "No, Liam."

"Oh," Liam says, clearly disappointed.

"My tigress, being who she is, always likes to be in control. She gets grumpy when I tether her, which, in turn, makes me grumpy," Celia explains. "And Taran, well, a lot makes her grumpy. Sometimes we clash, even though I recognize it's my tigress needling me and that I should be more patient. But as I mentioned, my tigress is hard to control."

"What do you fight about?"

She smiles fondly. "Stupid stuff really. Clothes, personal space. We don't have a lot of either and we all share the same bedroom."

"Why?" Liam asks.

Liam's question is fairly innocent. But Celia's life is more complex than most. It takes her a moment to gather her words, saying only enough to answer him. "Our foster mother doesn't have a lot of space in her house," Celia admits. "But that's okay. She loves us, and it shows in the way she cares for us."

Liam is clueless most of the time, but he's not dumb. The way Celia's voice fades and that sadness she keeps tucked away returns. She's done talking about her family.

Our original plan was to eat at my place, but as we reach the rear entrance to our property, I sense no one plans to stay.

"I need to make sure everyone is okay," Koda says. He backs away, waiting for the others to join him.

Liam kicks at the soil, bringing a small piece of moss into the air that he quickly catches. "I say after you check on the fam, you come and stay with me." He throws the piece of moss at Koda. It bounces off his chest. "Dad may need help fixing my neck, since Mom won't be able to hold me down."

Gratitude finds its way into Koda's voice. "All right. I'll be there."

"That was some fight today," Gemini says.

Koda grins. "Yeah. We owned it."

Gemini glances down, his cheeks flushing. "We all did well, but I was talking to Celia."

Koda nods, speaking to Celia. "I saw you flip and land a few times. It was—"

"Hot?" Liam offers.

Koda's hard gaze bounces to me. "I was going to say graceful," he mutters through his teeth.

"Oh. That, too," Liam agrees.

"My muscles are too heavy to do anything close to that," Koda continues. "You don't have that problem, Celia, even with all of your strength."

"You do have an impressive beast," Liam adds.

"Thank you," Celia says, looking intently at the ground.

She's not taken by the compliments or the attention my friends give her. They make her uncomfortable. It's one of the reasons I like her. She doesn't seek approval or demand everyone look at her, even though everyone does.

"We better head in," I say.

I wrap my arm around her shoulders and lead her forward. It's a natural response, but her tensing muscles make me think I shouldn't touch her. Not now. I turn around as the gate swings closed with a long-winded creak and drop my hand.

Gemini and Koda exchange glances. I'm not sure if they're upset that I touched her or that I let my arm fall away. And then there's Liam, giving me a double thumbs up. At least Liam thinks I'm doing something right, unlike the rest of us.

"By the way, cool underwear, Celia," Liam tells her.

"Excuse me?" she asks.

Liam beams. "Your underwear," he repeats. "I saw it when you flipped, kicked, and did that split. A little distracting, but awesome all the same."

"What?" he asks, when the wolves and I glare at him. "I like Wonder Woman."

"Goodnight, *Liam*," I say.

The sun had started its descent about a mile or two away. Like us, it seemed ready to end the day. On the mountain where I live, the best place to catch the sunset is on the terrace. As we walk up, bits of red and orange poke through the long branches, giving us a glimpse of what's to come.

I want to urge Celia forward so we can watch the final traces of light fade into the coming night. But her steps are slow, and her heart is heavy. I think I should make her laugh. Except, I'm a guy and not a very mature one.

I give Celia what I think is a playful nudge. With my wolf on edge following the fight, that show of affection is a lot harder than I intend. Celia falls on her side. The look on her face is comical, but neither of us is laughing.

"Did you just push me?"

"Ah. No?" I offer.

She kicks her legs in an arc and flips up into a standing position.

"Wow," I say.

She crosses her arms. "Is that all you have to say?"

I'm not wowed by her ability. What I am is blown away by *her*.

Celia is in a dress—a dress whose skirt raised up to give me another look at her lean legs—made strong by a beast she can barely control, who spent the day fighting alongside me and for *us*—and she just flips up—after I push her—and doesn't even go for my throat. Another female would be gnawing on my esophagus right about now.

"Aric?" she presses.

"Sorry?" I offer.

"For pushing me? For knocking me to the ground? Or for embarrassing me? You kind of did all three there, wolf."

Like an idiot, I smile. Seriously, that's all I've got.

Celia stares at me, her parting lips reflecting her shock. "You really aren't good with girls, are you?"

"Nope."

She places her hands on her hips. "I see."

She barely gets the last syllable out when she drops to the ground and sweeps her leg underneath mine. I don't just fall. My legs kick out and up, turning my normally smooth movements clumsy and dropping me like a newborn fawn.

Celia laughs. I almost do, too. I catch myself, pretending to be hurt.

"Ow," I moan, tightly clutching my ribs.

Celia hurries to my side. "I hurt you?"

I scrunch my face. "My beast is tired from battle and from everything he had to do to repair my crippled body."

I'm exaggerating the truth. Sure, I had some damage, but I was nowhere near crippled. I slowly relax my face, enough to be able to see Celia and to keep up my appearance of pain.

Her long hair falls to flutter against my shoulder and worry puckers her brow. Her eyes, *man*, I can look at those beauties forever.

"Aric," she says, her voice a gentle purr that strokes my skin in a lazy caress. "I'm so sorry. I had no idea *weres* could be injured like this from just a fall." She lifts my hand, clutching it between her breasts.

The warmth spreads between us and my eyes open and good *gawd*, why didn't I try this sooner?

Her gorgeous face consumes me. I'm barely able to form a single thought beyond kissing her. But then she bites down on her plump bottom lip and I know I'm done for.

"I didn't mean to hurt you," she stammers. I don't think she's embarrassed. I think she's speechless, like I am.

"I didn't mean to hurt you, either," I rasp. I motion behind her. "That push was supposed to be a love tap."

"A love tap?"

I groan. Way to ruin a moment.

"I meant tap. Just tap—a nudge." I groan, frustrated. "I was trying to be affectionate."

The corners of her mouth lift and she shakes her head like I'm the most pathetic male in the world, maybe because right now, I am. Around her, I'm clumsy and can barely string more than a few words together.

And I wouldn't want it any other way.

"There are other ways to show affection," she says, her sweet words stalling my heart.

She's close enough for me to lift up and kiss her. I think it's what she wants. I lick my lips, tilt my head to the side and . . . completely lose my nerve.

Instead, I playfully swipe mud on the tip of her nose. "You mean like this?"

She crinkles her nose in the cutest way possible and wipes her nose clean. "Or like this."

I'm too taken with Celia to see her hand coming at me. I make a face when she smears mud across my right cheek. "Aw, man," I say, laughing. "I'm going to get you for that one."

She's already on her feet, backing away. "You're going to have to catch me first, wolf."

Celia takes off with me in close pursuit. She's not as fast as she was earlier, the strain of battle slowing her down.

But she's still faster than me. Thing is, I'm determined to catch this little feline and sometimes that's all the incentive a wolf needs.

She sprints up the incline toward the house, running between the trees instead of taking the path. I should be telling her to slow down and to take it easy, or at least remind her that it's been a rough day and we need to rest and replenish our calories.

Instead, I run faster, encouraging her to quicken her speed. She thinks she knows where she's going, but she doesn't know this land like I do.

I cut right and then left at the barn, snagging Celia by the waist and spinning her. Her arms wrap around my neck and the world as I know it slows.

"No fair," she says, pretending to pout.

Her hair flows behind her and the bits of sunlight that remain cast a shimmer across her eyes. I smile. "Totally fair," I say.

I stop spinning and lift Celia into my arms. She kicks her feet as I walk to the back of the house and hop up the steps leading to the terrace. Given how strong she is, she could easily break free. I'm only holding her enough that she doesn't fall.

I carefully set her down when we reach the top. She smiles up at me, taking my hand and allowing me to lead her to the edge. I get my wish and watch the sunset with Celia wrapped in my arms.

The last streaks of red and orange vanish into the mountains, the sky proclaiming the day is done. Darkness encases us and the first few stars blink before we speak again. I should have taken her inside long before this, offered her a hot meal to beat back the cold the night brings, and water to settle the thirst making my voice sound raw. But these moments with Celia mean everything to me, and for the time being, the only peace I can offer.

My attention falls to our carefully clasped hands. It doesn't matter that we come from different worlds. We fit as easily as the moon among the stars.

"There's a dance at the end of the month to celebrate the Harvest Moon." I pause. "It's kind of a big deal around here. I think humans would refer to it as prom. We dress up and celebrate in the big hall." I look at her then. "Will you go with me?"

There are skinwalkers prowling our borders and natural disasters awoken by dark powers. We fought off a supernatural spell that sent scorpions to sprout from the ground like cabbage.

Bottom line. I'm a young male, holding a pretty girl close enough to kiss. Evil be damned. All I can think about is kissing Celia and taking her to prom.

Her lips part the way they do when she's surprised. "I don't know if I'll still be here," she says.

Yeah. About that . . .

My thumb passes between the grooves in her knuckles, the motion littered with all the grief I feel when I think about her leaving me. "I get it," I say. "But if you are, will you go with me? We can figure out shoes and a dress for you later and—"

"I would love to," she says, cutting me off with just a whisper.

The day my grandfather passed away was a moment I'll never forget. He died clutching my grandmother, who had died mere seconds before him. He didn't want to be without his mate, a gentle *were* who often told me she never knew happiness until she met Grandad. That memory is seared in my mind forever. It showed me what it is to love and how some just need each other to breathe, to smile, to live.

This moment with Celia is like that memory and one I pray I'll never forget.

I release her hand and draw her to me, my arms around her as the moon bathes us in its glow and the last of the birds fly home.

Chapter Sixteen

Last night was the best night of my life. Yeah, yeah, I get we almost died that afternoon. Still. It was amazing. My parents had come home while we were at Mimi's. Dad started up our generator enough so the power on the first floor would work and Mom could restock the fridge. Dad left another note, saying they'd be back by the end of week. He also asked about Celia.

No. He didn't know who she was or probably what she was. *I passed by your room*, he wrote. *New friend?*

Yeah. She is and, maybe, more.

When Celia and I walked in from the terrace, we snacked on food from the pantry. I started to get dinner going, but it was clear I didn't know what I was doing. Sure, I can roast prepared steaks over the fire well enough. But although there was plenty of food, I wasn't sure what to do with it.

"Can I cook for you?" she asked.

"Why?" I questioned, though me standing there awkwardly poking at the potatoes was answer enough.

She seemed embarrassed. I stood smiling like a fool. "I just want to do something nice for you," she said.

For all I knew, she was the world's worst cook. Still, I wasn't about to tell her no.

We showered while the roast with basil, potatoes, and carrots she prepared cooked in the oven. I finished my shower first and rushed downstairs. I set the table in front of the fireplace and placed some old Christmas lights I found in the basement along the hearth. I must have fiddled with the lights, and the candles I lit half a dozen times and racked my head with what kind of music to play. I settled on a classic rock station. The music was soft, but not too soft. I don't remember ever being this picky about anything. But I wanted to do something nice for her, too.

Celia came down in one of my mother's cotton dresses. This one was white and suited her well. It might have been too big in some spots for her small frame and, yeah, the hem skimmed her ankles instead of lying on her calves like it should. But it didn't make a difference. At least not to me.

She paused at the top of the stairs, biting her lip again when she caught sight of my widening eyes.

"What's this?" she asked, motioning around.

"Eh," was my response.

She averted her gaze and tried again. I tried, too, only I didn't get very far. "You were making dinner."

"So, you made me prom?" she offered when nothing else seemed to want to come out of my mouth.

I turned around and looked at my work. I'd covered the table with a white tablecloth and placed those long skinny candles Mom used for special dinners on top. I'd also laid out cloth napkins and arranged the silverware the way I thought it went and poured water into fancy glasses. The music played from the speakers near the hearth and the space between the hearth and the table was big enough to dance in.

"I guess I did," I answered.

Maybe there was a part of me that worried Celia would leave me before we'd make it to the dance. But I didn't want to think about it then. I just wanted to be with her.

Her bare feet padded across the wood floor. I smiled, wishing I could tell her how beautiful she is. I didn't manage, but I did ask her to dance after we finished an incredible meal.

The song was *Into the Mystic*. Van Morrison, I think. It was late, we were both acting shy, and aside from my mom, I'd never danced with another person.

"I only ever danced with my father," she admitted. "And that was a long time ago."

Somehow, we made it work.

My hand found her lower back as hers curved around the top of my shoulder. Our fingers linked, our gazes met, and we danced, her head falling against my chest and my arms encircling her into the next song and the one after that.

I walked her back to my room and said goodnight. This time when she closed the door, she didn't press furniture against it. She didn't even lock it.

It made it easy to do what we did next.

Rays of light beat against my closed eyelids, demanding I wake, instead of scrunching my face and turning away from the day. My bare chest slides against Celia's back.

Celia?

Whoa. I did it again.

I blink my eyes open, my nose twitching when her long hair tickles the tip. My arms are wrapped around her waist and my body is curled securely against hers. She's not pulling away or trying to hide. Instead, her arms rest over mine, keeping me close.

I'm not sure this is right, and I can't for the life of me remember how I got here. My conscience tells me I should slip away. I don't want her to feel scared, or to think I crawled into bed with her on purpose.

Slowly, I inch my arms away from hers, trying to be quiet and not rouse her from sleep. But when she purrs, I stop moving altogether, unable to stop my smile or the chuckle that follows.

"You're awake," she says.

Celia doesn't sound sleepy. She sounds content, her husky voice stirring my senses.

"And you're purring," I say, laughing when she does it again. "I thought big cats couldn't purr."

"They can't," she squeaks, embarrassed. "I told you, I'm weird."

My smile vanishes. *No, you're perfect.*

I adjust my hold, trying to keep it loose so she can scoot away if she'd like. I hope she doesn't. Her warmth and softness, they're heaven.

I press my forehead against the back of her head to remind her I'm here and how close our bodies are. It sounds like a stupid thing to do, but this is the first time she doesn't feel nervous having me so near.

Well, maybe not the first time. Last night, when we danced, that was pretty awesome.

Celia's presence is reassuring. I'm comfortable around her and want her to feel the same way. But I can't make her, nor do I want her to do anything she's not ready for.

"You wandered into my bed again," she says.

"No," I say. "I wandered into *my* bed."

"Okay. You wandered back into *your* bed with me in it and . . . fell asleep?"

"That sounds about right," I agree.

"You don't remember?" she asks.

"No. Do you?"

Her soft hair brushes against my cheek when she shakes her head. "I only remember waking up with you against me."

In a way, I wish we could remember. In other ways, this seems better. Innocent, I suppose, making our actions pure and not something we'll regret.

"Was it okay?" I ask. "Me being next to you like this?"

Her voice quiets. "It was the best thing ever."

"Ever?" I ask. I don't think she's crying, but I do hear the tears in her voice.

"Yes," she whispers.

I nuzzle her neck, wondering why my eyes sting the way that they do. "I feel the same."

The wind picks up outside, pushing the darkening clouds to cover what remains of the sunlight. A few birds skitter past the window and a few chirp further away. But the sound that takes up the room is our quiet breathing.

Our chests rise and fall in unison in the minutes that follow.

"Can I tell you something?" Celia asks. "Something that no one else knows?"

"You can tell me anything."

I mean what I say, and she seems to want to tell me. Still, it takes her a moment to answer. "I get scared a lot."

Her admission gives me pause. I think I know why, but I try to make sure. "Being here? With all this dark magic?"

"No. Being anywhere." She sighs. "So much has happened to me and to my sisters, Aric. We've helped each other through it and I've tried to be strong and make things right. But sometimes, it's so hard. And some days, I don't think I'll ever be enough."

"Celia." I want to offer words of comfort except they don't come.

"I don't know what's coming, Aric. I just know something is. Something bad. When it arrives, I may not be strong enough to stop it, or have what it takes to protect my family."

"You're not alone, Celia. We can protect your family together."

"You're sweet. But your life is here. Mine isn't. I have to go back, and it has to be soon. Regardless of what Mimi says, the only way to make sure my family is safe is for me to return."

I close my eyes, thankful that she can't see the grief plaguing my features. How can I make her understand that my life isn't anything without her in it? Two days. That's all I've known Celia. No time at all to fall as hard as I have, but here I am, falling further.

A wolf is only as good as his word. It's one of the first things Dad taught me. I promised to get Celia back to her home, but I no longer think it's a promise I can keep. Each moment that passes between us makes me think her home is here with me.

My thumb sweeps back and forth across her stomach, tracing invisible lines and swirls. I need Celia. I only wish she needed me, too.

She curls her spine, settling her body closer to me. She slept in that brown dress Mom wears when she tends to her herbs. It smells of sage and spearmint. Mostly it smells of Celia, kindness, beauty, and plenty of smarts. Someone who deserves happiness and maybe someone who can give it to her.

I sigh, pushing my selfish desires aside and focusing on what's right. "You'll get back to your family."

"When?" she asks.

I press a kiss against her shoulder and give her a squeeze. "Whenever we can manage it."

"Thank you," she says, her voice softening with what I interpret as hope. Hope that she makes it back to her family . . . or maybe hope for us.

I focus on the latter as silence overcomes the room. The outdoors isn't as quiet. The increasing sound of the wind beats against the pane, drowning out the caw of crows urgent to seek shelter.

My body relaxes from the feel of Celia so close, my immediate fear of losing her lessening. For now, she's here. For now, she's mine. So, for now, that's all I'll focus on.

"I'm not sure how this keeps happening," I say after a while. "Me showing up here, I mean."

"Mm-hmm."

I laugh. "You don't believe me?"

"Not even a little bit," she says.

"You should." We snuggle deeper beneath the blankets when the wind beats harder against the window.

"Why?" she asks.

I grin. She's all sorts of cute. "Because I don't want you afraid of me."

Her small nails skim across my forearms, delicately teasing the skin. Mini-bolts of energy surge along the pathways, causing my body to heat.

I shake off the feelings her touch causes, worried my desire will scare her like it scares me.

"I'm afraid of a lot of things," she reminds me, the heaviness in her tone reflecting the kind of life she's had. "But you're not one of them."

Relief floods me in languid ripples. "Good."

"So," she begins after a moment. "You have no idea how you got here?"

"I have some idea."

"You do?" she asks.

"Yeah. You see, it started off when my mother and father fell in love and got married. After a while they thought, hey, we need a really cool kid to complete our family. So, one night—"

She nudges me playfully in the stomach, both of us laughing. "That's enough out of you." I can't see her face, but I feel her smile like a ray of sunshine straight into my heart. "You're doing this on purpose and blaming your actions on your poor wolf."

"I swear I'm not." I wonder if I should come clean about how I feel or if I'm better off shutting my trap. Ultimately, I swing open the trap and let it all come out. "If I was coming in here on purpose, would you mind?"

Celia stills in my arms. For a second, I'm sure I've gone too far. "Mind waking up next to you?" she asks.

"Yeah," I answer almost silently.

The comforter and sheets rustle as she turns to face me. Her expression gives away her fear and, in her scent, I sense her apprehension. But her large eyes, the same eyes that shimmer when she laughs, reflect what I'm feeling. "No," Celia whispers. "I wouldn't mind."

I cup her face and kiss her. There's nothing slow about it. Not like in the movies. There's no soft music to set the mood, or a buildup of sound to mirror the fear and excitement I feel. There's just me capturing her mouth with mine.

My lips slide against hers while my fingertips graze down her cheek. I almost expect her to pull away and insist I'm doing it all wrong. I'm no expert. Instead, she welcomes my mouth, seeking as much of me as she can take.

My heart brutalizes my chest in the best way possible. I'm out of breath when we finally part and I'm not sure I remember my name. Like I said, I used to be cool. Now, all I am is head over heels for Celia.

The smile she greets me with makes the kiss and every moment we've shared alone that much sweeter.

My thumb passes across her jaw. "Was that all right?" I ask. I zero in on her full lips, wanting more than anything to return to them. "I've never done that before."

"Never?" she asks.

My gaze travels over her face, taking in her thick lashes, her glistening eyes, and the almost invisible freckle on her cheek. That confidence I'm known for never seems to make an appearance around Celia in moments like this. I play with the strands of her hair, trying to disguise my nervousness and doing a lousy job. I didn't feel us move much when we kissed, but the way her head of curls fans around us, I suppose we did.

"I was never really interested in females." I meet her eyes. "Until now."

Celia blinks several times. For a second, I'm sure she's going to cry. I glance away, unable to bear it. "What about you? Have you kissed a lot of males?"

Why did I ask? Based on how good it was, Celia has experience and knows what she's doing.

Celia's cheeks flush with embarrassment and with what, God help me, resembles longing. "There's only one boy I've ever kissed."

I press my jaw tight. I suppose it was too much to hope for. "Oh," I mutter. "Sorry. I guess I shouldn't be so surprised."

Her hand slides over mine when I try to pull away. "Do you want to know his name?"

So I can hunt him down and break his legs? Sure. I shrug. "You can tell me if you want."

"Are you sure?" She taps her chin, appearing to give it some thought. "You look a little mad there, wolf."

"Positive," I grumble. It's one of those moments where I'm glad Celia can't sniff a lie.

Her features soften, erasing her playful nature, and her voice is nothing more than a gentle stream of words. "His name is Aric and . . . I think I love him."

I can't breathe. Can't move. Can't . . . "What?"

She laughs, since I'm obviously not embarrassed enough. "You're incredible," she says, the flush in her cheeks spreading across her face and beyond. "I've never met anyone so perfect."

My wolf leaps inside me, running around in circles. This is the moment to be romantic and to say something that will blow her away. Instead, I kiss her, showing her with my lips everything I can't say with my mouth.

Celia falls onto her back, her fingers dragging through my hair as my arms band around her waist. This is greatest moment of my life.

"*Aric!*"

Until Mom's voice from the doorway tells me it's over.

I jump up into a sitting position, my eyes wild when I see Mom *and Dad* standing in the doorway.

"I thought you weren't coming home until Friday?"

Dad takes my comment as well as you might think. "*Is that all you have to say right now?*"

"Uh."

Mom gasps, covering her mouth, her gaze travelling between me and Celia. "Oh, my God," she says.

Dad stands frozen. That doesn't mean I can't sense the underlying rage surging to the surface. He takes a step forward. "Didn't you tell me, just the other day, that you didn't even notice girls?" he asks, his tone clipped.

I slide out of bed, wearing only the basketball shorts I slept in. I glance at Celia as she slithers out of the bed and toward the window, her face flaming as red as mine feels.

I clear my throat. "This probably looks bad—"

"*You think?*"

Dad is raging. I can count on one hand how many times Dad has growled at me in my life. This is one of them. Trust me when I say, it makes up for the rest.

He storms forward, his face reddening. "We leave you alone for two days only to find you bedding a young female you should know better than to disrespect."

"Dad, it's not like that—"

"What's it like, Aric?" he snaps. "She's young. Impressionable. You had no right taking advantage of her innocence."

Dad has written Celia off as one of those naive girls only interested in me for my family's status. It makes me angry. Not because he thinks I somehow used my clout, but because of what he thinks I did to her.

"I would never take advantage of Celia!"

My growls only further enrage Dad's wolf. "Then what do you call this?" he asks, his deep voice booming. "This isn't her first time in your room. I sensed her in here yesterday, but I had no idea *this* was happening."

"There is no 'this'," I insist. "Not in the way that you're thinking."

"We found you in bed with a female, Aric. Do you have any idea how insolent your actions are? This is our home. A sacred place. You've barely stepped into adulthood and this is the activity you're engaged in?" He points at Mom. "Your *mother* saw you like this."

His voice cuts off and his hand slowly lowers when he sees Mom standing in front of Celia.

Celia practically has her foot out the window. She probably meant to make her big escape. Mom held her in place. Not with her hands. Mom wouldn't threaten an innocent like Celia, but with the way she responds to Celia.

Mom's eyes brim with tears as her hands fall away from her mouth. "Celia," she says, inching forward. Very carefully, she reaches out, smoothing Celia's long hair around her shoulder.

Celia's gaze follows Mom's every motion. Her breath hitches as Mom shows her affection only a real mother can demonstrate. I don't have to guess it reminds Celia of her own mother. I can see it in her stance. She's remembering the feel of those long-forgotten touches.

Mom sniffs, turning around to face Dad as the first of her tears fall. "Her name is Celia, Aidan."

There's nothing left of Dad's rage. The shock he initially demonstrated returns ten-fold.

"My God," he says. "How is this possible? He's too young."

My face falls briefly into my hands. "We didn't do anything," I repeat.

I make my way to Celia, worried I abandoned her. I reach for her, wishing that gentle warmth her touch causes didn't result in waves of butterflies fluttering up my spine. Not in front of my parents.

"Celia is in trouble," I say. "I found her in the forest the day I went hunting." I clear my throat twice. "She's my girlfriend now and she needs me."

Dad places his arm around Mom. It's then I realize there's more to their reactions than what appears on the surface.

When Dad speaks, I know my world will change forever.

"She's not your girlfriend," he says. "Aric, you found your mate."

Chapter Seventeen

I start to speak, ready to deny it and accuse Dad of reading too much into it. But my wolf is doing backflips inside of me, lunging at my chest, excited I finally understand what he's been trying to tell me.

Instead of arguing, I squeeze Celia's hand, trying to reassure her that this isn't so bad and that, maybe, it's actually perfect.

The joy spreading through me is like a breath of fresh air I wasn't aware I needed to take.

"Whoa," I say, vaguely aware that I'm smiling.

"I'm sorry," Celia says. "I don't understand what this means. I'm not like you."

"Celia isn't like anyone," I explain. "She's unique. A special being unlike anyone else in existence."

"I gathered that much," Mom says.

Mom isn't judging Celia. Like the rest of us, she recognizes Celia is different. Yet even knowing Celia is a non-pure *were*, she's welcoming of Celia's presence. It means everything to me.

As mated *weres* themselves, my parents understand Celia's importance and they are genuinely happy for me. But all isn't well with the world, and the next few moments are harsh reminders.

The wind bangs like a fist against the window. Leaves that should remain firmly in place along the trees sweep by as if torn from their branches.

Dad's narrowing gaze fixes on the window and beyond. "Aric," he says. "Help me bring down the storm shutters. I want to preserve the generator's power."

"What's happening?" I ask.

Dad doesn't hesitate to answer. "The dark magic we've hunted has dispersed from the borders and scattered around the state. It's closing in around us and we're not sure where it will strike next."

The muscles around my spine grow rigid, squaring my shoulders. "It'll strike here, Dad. This darkness, it's coming for Celia."

Dad and I secured the windows and doors with the metal shutters. We then tightly locked up the barn. I tell him as much as I can in the short time we work. We walk inside about an hour later to find Mom and Celia cooking in the kitchen and softly speaking. The wind sweeps inside before Dad can finish closing us in, fluttering the skirt of Mom's pink dress around her legs.

Mom gave Celia another set of clothes, a blue shirt that hangs off her shoulders and white shorts. They fit her perfectly. I smile when she looks up from where she's helping Mom cut up vegetables.

Seeing Celia like this in my kitchen, I suddenly can't remember a time when she wasn't with me. She returns my smile, but it doesn't last. Worry crinkles her brow. As much as I want to smooth it away with a kiss, this isn't the time. Too much is coming and those I most love are in danger. We need to form a plan.

We talk about the last few days over lunch, each detail of Celia's arrival thickening the air around us as the harsh winds continue to pummel the house.

Dad tightly holds Mom's hand where they sit across from us. I hold tight to Celia's, waiting for Dad to provide some insight and maybe the hope we need.

He drags his hand down his face, something he does when he's frustrated, and the answers aren't coming.

"There's a lot that doesn't sit well with me," he says. "It's not just Celia's arrival and the darkness her presence brought here. It's the timing."

"What do you mean?" I ask, knowing he's going somewhere I won't like.

"It's a rare thing for *weres* to meet their mates this young," Mom explains, offering Celia a gentle smile. "It's not that we don't welcome you, dear, or the happiness you will bless our son with. It's simply that matehood at your age shouldn't be possible."

"I apologize," Celia says. "I'm trying to understand. But I'm not familiar with your ways."

"I'm familiar," I interject. "And I'm still confused." I suppose I should know, but I never cared about matehood enough to ask. My parents are mates and that's all that mattered. Until now. "I've heard *weres* can find their mates as young as eighteen, but more often in their early twenties. Why, if their souls are meant to connect for eternity?"

"It has to do with breeding," Dad replies. He leans forward, his white T-shirt stretching across his broad chest. Dad isn't one to mince words, but I can tell he's uncomfortable saying what he does in front of Celia. "For centuries, our numbers were few. We'd become an endangered species. Then something changed. Either our beasts adapted, or nature adapted them for us. *Weres* began finding mates later, the maturity of their bodies resulting in stronger offspring and more *weres* to strengthen our numbers."

"Revitalizing our race," I infer.

"Exactly," Dad agrees.

"Is that what has you so upset?" I ask. "I mean, it's not like Celia and I are looking to breed."

I regret the words as soon as they shoot out of my mouth. If it weren't for me holding Celia's hand, I think she'd disappear under the table.

Dad just smiles. It's not a friendly smile. "You're right about that, *son*."

Mom pushes around what remains of the pie she baked with her fork. "I'm wondering if we should move Celia's room closer to ours and perhaps redo the barn to give Aric his own space?"

"What?" Celia asks. She glances around. "You're inviting me to stay here permanently?"

I'm not sure who's more stunned, me or Celia. Dad winks at Mom. "Mates have a hard time keeping away from each other, sweet one."

"I can't stay," Celia says. "My family needs me."

Dad nods. "Aric told me the circumstances surrounding your family. But you must understand, your bond with Aric is too strong to permit you to go so far away. Look at the way you woke together, and you were merely a few rooms away. In another state, it would be unbearable." He works his jaw. "And with what I feel stirring in those winds, you'll need our protection and so will your family."

"My foster mother, Ana Lisa, is very sick," Celia says slowly. "She needs a great deal of care."

"And she'll find it here with us, child," Dad tells her gently. "You're Aric's family. That makes you our family, and your family will be ours, as well."

I'm ready for Celia to agree to all of it. But her pride and circumstances get in the way. "This is a lot to consider and it's not my decision alone," she says. "It's not that I want to leave Aric, but I need to take care of my family first and see to their needs. We're really struggling, and Ana Lisa's insurance is based in New Jersey."

I never told Celia my family and I come from a great deal of wealth. Mom does it for me, more elegantly than I ever could.

"You won't have to struggle here," Mom says. "We'll make certain Ana Lisa receives the best care in the local hospitals and beyond. There's a healing witch not too far from here. She won't be able to cure Ana Lisa. Magic works with magic and as a human, your dear foster mother has none to spare. But she can ease her pain and possibly improve her outcome."

"You're very kind," Celia says, glancing around. "All of you. But I can't ask you to pay for her medical costs."

"You're not asking, child," Dad says. "We're offering, and we will gladly manage everything, including the move." He looks at Mom. "I like your idea of giving Aric his own space. But if we reconstruct the barn, we can give Celia and our new family their own home."

Celia doesn't speak. The tears filling her eyes say enough.

Dad's expression softens, but soon worry overtakes it. "There is much to do and discuss with regards to your family. But our first priority is figuring out your situation and making certain you stay safe." He rises. "I'll summon Mimi. Perhaps she has found the answers we need." He makes a face. "Although, I would have preferred it if you'd gone to Bellissima."

My gaze falls on Celia. I would have preferred a lot of things. "I didn't think I could."

"Ordinarily, it would go against our ways," Dad agrees. "But these are extraordinary times."

And Celia is an extraordinary person, I don't bother adding.

"Leave those, dears," Mom says when Celia and I start to clear the table. "This is more important, and it won't take long."

Dad reaches into the fireplace and scoops up a mound of ash between his palms. He steps backward and into the space where Celia and I danced the night before, sprinkling the ash in a circle as he speaks.

"Mimi," he says. "Wild Hag of the Whispering Mountains, Guardian of the Owls, Granddaughter of Ahanu the Great Bear. I, Aidan Connor, Leader, Alpha, and pureblood, summon thee to my home."

He closes the circle. "Come forth in peace and leave in peace." He brings his foot down, slamming it hard. I ease Celia behind me, expecting a big explosion of light and power with the summoning.

It doesn't come.

The circle Dad created glows with faint light, solidifying the *call,* but then, nothing. He looks up at us. "Mimi," he bellows. "I summon thee. Appear."

Again, he slams his foot. Again, the circle glows with that faint light. But that's it.

"Something's wrong," Mom says, standing.

Dad edges away from the circle, watching it as if expecting answers within the space.

He looks up at Celia, his expression wrought with worry. "Celia," he says. "What day is it?"

"Sunday," Celia offers.

"No," Dad says. "It's Wednesday."

I don't like his tone. Not for a simple mistake like this. My heartbeat pounds in miserable and angry strikes. "She lost track of the days, that's all," I reason.

Dad abandons the circle completely, walking slowly toward us and stopping in front of Celia. "Child," he says, trying to keep his voice calm. "How old are you?"

"I'm fifteen, sir."

Dad sighs, appearing relieved. "And what time of year is it?"

"Summer, sir. Almost fall."

Panic threatens to choke me. "Celia," I say, carefully. "It's May."

Her eyes widen and she releases my hand, stepping away.

"Don't," I say. "It's okay."

She startles when she bumps into Mom. Mom holds her gently. "Aidan?" Mom says. "What's happening?"

My dad closes his eyes and releases a long breath. When he opens them, he's not any less fearful. "Child," he says to Celia. "What year is it?"

My stomach bottoms out when Celia answers two years from now. "She's just confused," I interrupt. "We fought a skinwalker and those scorpions. She could have hit her head."

"I didn't hit my head, Aric," Celia replies. "You know I didn't."

Yeah. I do. But this . . . this is so wrong.

I walk away, dragging my hand through my hair. I don't understand what's happening, but I recognize things are worse than I could have imagined.

Mom smooths Celia's hair, trying to reassure her when Dad tells her the year.

"What?" Celia asks, close to tears. "How am I here in the past? In a season and place very different from my own?"

"Because you don't belong here," Mimi croaks behind us. "Not now. Not with Aric."

Mimi sits in the circle, her cloak dripping with blood and pieces of red-soaked plumage stuck in her hair. Her face is bruised and she's clutching her limp arm against her chest.

Dad jets to Mimi's side, lifting her and placing her small, damaged body on the couch.

Mom covers Mimi with a blanket, carefully examining her broken arm. Mimi's breathing is shallow, and her skin is the color of her gray, crooked teeth. The hysterical and psychotic cackles so associated with her personality are notably absent, as is the insane amount of power that marks her as a formidable hag.

I barely get the words out. "What happened?"

Mimi manages to speak, but the effort costs her. She grimaces in pain. "I told you they'd come after the tigress and anyone linked to her." She smiles. "They found me first and now, they come for the rest."

Celia clutches my arm. "Aric, that means they'll go after Gemini, Liam, and Koda."

"And those they hold most dear," Mimi finishes for her. She stares blankly at the ceiling, the life in her eyes fading fast. "No one who helped her is safe."

Dad wrenches to his feet, racing to the door. He throws open the storm shutter leading out to the terrace and barrels through. I'm right behind him, moving so fast I almost trip over his feet.

The wicked wind and debris it carries cuts into our faces. To the far east and west, lightning crashes and several dark twisters take form. Their thin shapes bang into each other like vicious warriors, desperate to find what they seek.

To the north, about twenty miles away, the ground begins to quake, sending boulders crashing down the mountain.

Dad howls, *calling* for my friends. I join him, throwing my head back and using all the breath I can manage. Celia referred to our *calls* the other night as beautiful. These are far from that. They're angry, demanding their presence and warning them of the danger.

We wait for several long minutes. But only the fury of the twisters and quakes can be heard.

Dad and I try again. Nothing but our howls ring out. As their Alpha, they're obliged to answer Dad unless they can't.

"Dad? Why aren't they answering? Why isn't *any* wolf answering?"

"In times like this when evil rises, my *weres* know to join their packs and seek refuge."

"But they should respond, at the very least to let you know they're safe," I bite out.

His thick white hair flutters in the breeze. "I know, Aric."

Chapter Eighteen

Rage tightens Dad's stance. He thinks they're dead and he's not alone.

"Aric? Mr. Conner?"

I whip around to see Celia, standing in the doorway. "Your mother wants you both inside."

We don't waste any time. I help Dad bring down the metal shutter just as something hard crashes against it, denting it inward and preventing us from closing the door.

Mom has Mimi sitting up, helping her sip on tea with leaves floating on the top. I recognize that tea. The healing witch Mom spoke of gave it to her to treat those of magic injured in her absence. It's probably the only reason Mimi remains conscious.

Mimi's cloak lies in a clear bag near the side table. She's wearing a white nightgown and her long, matted hair falls around her in thick clumps. Someone attempted to brush through it, until they saw the ugly gash along her scalp.

Mom and Celia saw quickly to Mimi. But she's still close to death. For the moment, she's awake, and given her state, it's an absolute miracle.

Celia edges away so Dad can kneel beside Mom. I gather Celia so her back presses against my chest, kissing her cheek and hugging her close.

"The wolves didn't answer you, did they?" she asks.

I want to assure her they will. But I won't give her false hope. It's not what any of us needs now. "No."

"Great Mimi," Dad says. "I beg your forgiveness for what I request of you at this time. But for the sake of my pack, I implore you to tell me what's happening."

A crazed expression overtakes Mimi's features. She attempts to smile, but doesn't quite manage, moaning in pain and clutching her arm. Her voice is a shadow of what it once was, but I understand her well enough. What follows isn't anything I'm prepared to hear.

"Alpha, your pleas for forgiveness are not needed, but your strength for what I must tell you is." She motions to my mother for more healing tea. Mom holds her head as Mimi takes several greedy gulps. Mom attempts to dab Mimi's lips when she finishes, but Mimi bats Mom's hand away. Mimi doesn't want to be fussed over. What little energy she has is needed for her to speak.

"The little tigress must survive," Mimi says. "Everything good in the world tells me it must be so."

Mimi's eyes lower and she appears to fall asleep.

"Why?" Dad asks. He shakes Mimi gently. "Stay with us, great hag, and explain your reasoning."

Mimi blinks open her eyes. Mom offers her more tea. Mimi takes it down as if dying of thirst. But thirst isn't what ails her.

"The tigress is special, as are her sisters," Mimi continues, tea dribbling out of her mouth. "For the dark ones to triumph, evil cannot allow her to live."

Mimi swallows a few times, as if she's drinking tea, even though none is offered. Her dull gaze drifts to Celia, the effort causing her more pain. "Good knows you're needed, just as it knows evil needs you dead. It alerted the light witch, but she was untrained and ill-connected with her gifts. She followed you, intent on warning you. But then the dark witches arrived."

"She couldn't fight them," Mimi continues, her voice stuttering. "She was outmatched in skill and supremacy. She realized as much and cast the only spell she could to keep you safe."

"The one that sent me here."

Celia's voice is so quiet, I'm not sure how Mimi hears her. "Yes," Mimi replies. "To the one being who will forever protect you and share your soul."

Mom's head drops into her hand. "But it's not the right time," she says.

"No," Mimi agrees. "The light witch's spell was powerful, but untamed. It spiraled out of control, surging in strength, instead of dwindling. It fed the ley lines and forced them to shift."

"What are ley lines?" Celia asks.

She already knows it's bad news. I barely have the nerve to answer. "Magical lines that run throughout the earth and in conjunction with fault lines."

Mimi quickly takes more tea when Mom presses the cup against her cracked lips. "It triggered the earthquakes and summoned dark storms and weather, altering and mismatching periods of time, and stirring creatures meant to huddle in darkness." She chuckles without humor. "Creatures the dark ones were more than pleased to use in their favor to hunt the tigress."

Mom turns to Dad. I've never seen her so devastated. "That's how they located Celia, Aidan. These dark witches may reside in the future, but unlike the light witch, they're able to control their power. They used the spell meant to spare Celia to their advantage."

Mom looks at me then, her eyes spilling with tears when she catches how close I'm clutching Celia. "Do you understand, Aric? The dark witches can't hunt Celia from the future, but they don't have to. They merely had to latch onto the spell the light witch cast and compel the dark powers it awakened to kill Celia for them."

My gut twists so badly it's hard to remain standing. It all makes sense. But it's not over.

Celia isn't crying. Not yet. But she's close. "What happened to the light witch who tried to help me?"

Dad shakes his head. "An untrained witch matched against three who were? Nothing good," he answers.

"As I told you, little tigress," Mimi murmurs. "She can't help you now."

I'm ready to tear this room apart. "Can you help Celia?" I ask. "Please, Mimi. You said it yourself, she has to survive."

Mimi's mouth falls open and several gasps of air follow. She's done for. I'm sure of it. It's just a matter of time.

Mom pours more tea into Mimi's mouth. Most of it pools, the rest spilling over the sides. I expect Mimi to choke on what remains, but it just sits there. Mom whispers in Mimi's ear, her voice barely a touch of sound, unlike the magic that Mom's beast stirs inside of her.

"Great and powerful Mimi, for the sake of our son and his mate, give us direction. Tell us what to do."

Mimi's head slumps to the side, the residual tea pouring from her mouth and onto the couch. I think she's dead, but then she smiles, and I just about lose my mind.

"I can't cast a spell to change time or conjure one to take place in the future," Mimi mumbles. "But I can alter a spell that continues to brew."

"To do what exactly?" I growl.

"To send Celia back," Mimi slurs.

The wind pummels the side of the house as I all but snap my teeth at her. "*No*."

"Aric," Mom says. "We have to listen to what Mimi has to say."

I step in front of Celia, my voice catching when her arms band around my waist and her body presses against my back. Her shoulders shake as she sobs, causing my eyes to burn.

Why is this happening? *Why are they doing this to us?*

"Mimi can't take Celia away from me. There *has* to be another way."

Mimi's eyes narrow, her patience growing thin. Despite her weakening state, her voice turns firm. "If you want your mate to live—if you want her to accomplish everything the Power of Good expects of her, she *must* go back. There's no other way, young wolf."

"She's my *mate*," I say. "I can't lose her like this!"

"Aric," Dad begins.

"No," I interrupt. "You said it yourself, Dad. Mates don't do well being apart. Celia and I couldn't sleep a few feet away without finding a way to be next to each other. And now, you're not just talking about sending her to another state, you're talking about banishing her to the future, somewhere I may never find her again."

Something collides with the roof, rattling the house and creating a crack in the ceiling. It splinters down, all the way to floor, the motion so forceful the house shifts.

Dad gathers my mother against him, his cold stare briefly darting my way. "Make him forget about her," he orders Mimi. "Make them both forget."

"I don't want to forget!" I holler.

"I *can't* forget Aric," Celia says, her voice quivering with sadness. "It isn't possible."

"If it means your sanity, your heart, and your future, you both can and will." Dad rises. "Do you think I want to ask this of you? I know what it means to have a mate—"

"Then you know you're asking the unbearable," I say, cutting him off.

Dad takes a breath, relaxing his shoulders, unlike mine which carry all the rage I feel. "This isn't just about you and Celia, Aric. Did you not hear Mimi's words? This spell, however good its intention, has disrupted life as we know it. For Celia to survive and take her place along those who protect the earth, she has to go back."

Something else strikes the roof. It's not as loud or as strong, but it doesn't have to be. The damage is already done.

"You're asking Mimi to send Celia back to the same witches trying to kill her," I yell. "How is she supposed to help the world if she's already dead?"

"That's not what I'm asking Mimi to do," Dad says. "Celia was in an alley, in a city, correct?"

I don't want to answer, but I nod anyway.

He returns his full attention to Mimi. "Change the spell so that instead of sending her here, it sends Celia and her prey to a different part of the city."

"So, the light witch's spell never gets the chance to alter time," Mimi deduces. She cackles. It's faint, but there. "You ask a great deal, my Alpha. Especially from an old hag whose time has come."

"Can you do it?" Dad asks, his attention frantically scanning her frail state.

"I can," Mimi says.

"No, *no*." I turn around, digging my fingers through my hair only for my gaze to fasten on Celia. My hands fall to my sides when I see her red swollen eyes.

"Baby," I say, wrapping my arms around her. A knot forms in my throat, making it hard to speak. "We were supposed to be happy. You were supposed to live here with me. You, your family. You were never supposed to leave me."

"I don't want to leave you," Celia says, choking back a sob. "But you need to live, and you need to find me. Do you hear me? You and your wolf have to find a way back to me and my tigress."

"No," I insist. "I can't risk letting you go. What if I can't find you? What if you find someone else?"

"I *won't*," Celia says, crying so hard she can barely speak. "You'll always be the one."

Agony overtakes me, splitting my heart. I clutch her against me. Never have I felt so much pain.

"It's not so easy," Mimi mumbles as if my insides aren't being ripped from me. "Magic comes at a price. Neither good nor evil can prevail without payment."

Dad rises, his expression as dark as his voice. "And what is the price we must pay?"

Mimi lifts a weary finger in my direction. "A love like this can't merely be forgotten. The sacrifice of one must be replaced by another."

Dad doesn't hesitate. "I'll carry the burden of the memory," he says. "And sacrifice what's needed."

"*Aidan*," Mom cries.

"Wait, Dad—what are you doing?"

"I can handle the extent of your memories, feelings, all of it," Dad interrupts. "And whatever else is needed for Celia's safe return."

"Let me at least take part—"

"No," Dad says, interrupting Mom. "That's not an option. Your soul is tender, and this requires more steel than you can offer." He turns to Mimi. "Tell me what needs to be done."

"I don't want you to do this," Mom growls, rising.

Dad's voice remains gentle. "There's no choice. We're obliged to protect the world and if Celia has somehow been chosen to save it, we're obliged to save her. Not just for our son. But for all who inhabit it."

"Aidan," Mom says, crying into her hands.

Dad kisses her forehead. "It must be done, my love."

A howl erupts in the distance. We whip toward the barricaded door. "It's Liam," I say, knowing he's in trouble.

Mimi gags on her cackles. "They're coming for you, little tigress."

Dad drops to her side. "Mimi, tell me what to do."

"Tell me!" he yells when she falls unconscious.

Something strikes the door and dark red blood spills in from the outside. I charge to the metal door, throwing it open.

Koda's body falls at my feet, gripping the nape of Gemini's twin wolf. Neither are breathing. Koda is missing most of his right leg and pink fluid oozes from his mouth. The twin wolf's spine pokes out from his back and his blank stare faces the ceiling.

"*No!*"

Celia and I drag them inside. She feels for a pulse at Koda's neck and then Gemini's twin. It's too late. Their souls are already gone.

Liam howls again. "Help me!" he yells. "*Help me.*"

Mom *changes*, her clothes tearing from her body as her honey and cinnamon colored wolf emerges. She leaps over the dead bodies of my friends and over the railing, her snarls resonating as she slams into something at the bottom.

Through the howling wind, the stench of decay rises, singeing my nose. Another skinwalker has appeared and Mom is fighting it alone.

"Dad—"

My voice lodges in my throat as my father takes a large knife and stabs it through Mimi's chest. Mimi arches her back, cackling as Dad steps away. He marches toward us, careful not to spill the blood smearing the blade.

"Take this," he says to Celia. "Don't wipe it. Don't do anything. Step into the circle of ash, cut your palm with the tip, and Mimi's magic will do the rest."

With shaking hands, Celia takes the knife.

Dad places his hands on Celia's shoulders and presses a kiss to her forehead. "You won't be forgotten, sweet one. I swear it."

His head snaps up when he hears Mom yelp. In one motion, my father *changes* into his dark menacing wolf, leaping from the terrace and joining my mother. I sprint toward the railing, the wind so strong and littered with debris, I can barely see below.

What I do see is more than enough.

Liam's naked body lies unmoving below, his decapitated head several feet away from him. What remains of my friend is disintegrating from the skinwalker's poison. Like the other skinwalker, this one is more a decomposing corpse than anything living.

His face is that of a man combined with a horse, long with glowing humanoid eyes and a protruding lower jaw. Snakes replace his limbs and a forked tongue slithers out as he hisses. Mom and Dad circle him, leaping away from the poison on his limbs and desperate for a chance to bring him down.

I swing my foot over the rail, ready to pounce, but then a wave of magic kicks my leg out from under me. I leap into a crouch, recognizing the magic is Mimi's and that it's coming from the house.

Dad snaps his jaws, urging me inside. I back away, conflicted, only for another wave of magic to strike.

I bolt back into our large, open family room. Celia stands inside the circle of ash, staring at the gash in her palm. She looks up, dropping the knife Dad gave her when she sees me. It falls with *clang* against the floor.

"I have to go, Aric," she says, tears soaking her eyes. "You need to live and so do those you cherish."

"Mimi," I rumble. "Don't take her from me. There has to be another way!"

But Mimi is gone. There's nothing left of her but the white nightgown she wore and the spilled contents of the healing tea seeping from the shattered cup on the floor.

Something hideous bashes against the roof as Mom and Dad race back inside, their wolf forms panting hard from the fight . . . and from the poison eating through their flesh.

The skinwalker throws himself against the protection spells surrounding the house, screeching in a way that jolts the walls. Dad manages to roll the metal shutter down with his fangs.

Neither the door nor the spells will hold for long. I know it. Just as I know my parents don't have long to live.

White light soars from the circle, encasing Celia and bleaching her features. I throw myself against it, pounding on the ward created by the light.

"Celia!" I holler. "*Celia*!"

The strong arms of my father grab me, pulling me back. I lunge forward, breaking away from him and smashing through the ward. I snatch Celia's hands as she begins to disappear, my rage-filled tears making it hard to see.

Evil wasn't meant to awaken like this.

Death was not supposed to claim my friends and family.

It was the worst time to fall in love. But I did.

And it was worth every *fucking* moment.

But now, to save us all, I have to let the one being who shares my soul go.

No matter how much it destroys me.

"I'll find you," I tell Celia. "I swear, my wolf will stay with you and we will find a way."

I haul her to me, kissing her one last time before she fades away and all that's left is darkness.

Chapter Nineteen

I hop downstairs. I don't mean I take the steps one by one, or even three at a time. I mean hop over the railing and leap from the second floor to the first, landing almost silently in a crouch, the backpack on my shoulders barely brushing against my spine.

"Aric," Mom calls, turning away from the stove. "You're a *were*, not an animal. Take the stairs as you're supposed to."

"Sorry, Mom." I look around, noting breakfast is almost ready. "Where's Dad?"

"He said he had something to do outside." Mom brings a few dishes over. "Don't even think about it," she says when she sees me eyeing the bacon.

Dad chuckles as he walks into the house, pocketing the Swiss Army knife he's carrying into his jeans. He reaches for Mom, holding her close, but his attention is on me. "How'd you sleep?"

"Pretty good," I say. I wait just long enough for Dad to sit before attacking the bacon.

"Good," he says.

My knife slices into the butter when Mom drops several pancakes on my plate. The scent of cheese, carefully diced onions, and minced garlic seeps into my nose in a mouth-watering sweep when she returns with the eggs. The moment the first scoop lands on my plate, I dig in.

Dad hoists Mom onto his lap. "Eat with me," he tells her. "You're doing too much."

Mom kisses his cheek and places the pan on the table, but instead of letting Dad feed her, she wraps her arms around his neck. Her shoulder length white hair brushes against his chest and her eyes close with longing.

"You're hunting again, aren't you?" I ask.

Dad smiles softly at Mom when she cuddles closer, stroking her hair until she opens her eyes. She doesn't return his smile. It bothers me to see her so upset. "What's going on?" I ask.

"There's a dark witch causing trouble in Lesotho," Dad replies, continuing his slow caress of Mom's hair.

I reach for more bacon and eggs. "Where's that?"

"Africa," Mom replies. "It's a territory known for diamond smuggling and dark magic."

"Cue the witch," I guess. I shove a forkful of eggs down my throat and stab a few more pieces of bacon. "How'd you get wind of her?" I ask.

"She's protecting the diamond smugglers," Dad explains.

"Can I go with you?" I ask.

"No," Dad answers, something odd in his tone. "I need you here to look after your mother. I leave this afternoon, but I hope to return by the end of the week if all goes well."

"Oh." I play around with what little food remains on my plate. "Are you sure I can't go?"

"I'm sure," Dad says, his features wrought with sadness. "Your mother is worried enough, especially with all those females seeking your company."

I roll my eyes. The females I know are annoying at best, looking to get with me for all the wrong reasons. "I don't even like them."

Dad watches me as I rise to dump my plate in the sink.

"Where are you off to?" Dad asks.

"I'm going hunting," I reply. "Liam swears he scented elk near Mount Elbert."

Dad places Mom carefully on the floor as he rises. I brush my wet hands against my jeans, hugging him tight. "Good luck, Dad," I tell him.

"You too, Aric."

He releases me as the familiar voices of my friends sound from the front of the house. Excitement builds through me. It's going to be a great day.

"Gotta go," I say. I clap my dad's shoulder affectionately. "I'll see you at the end of the week."

Dad nods, gathering my mother against him when she wraps her arms around his waist.

"Son?"

Something in my father's voice keeps me in place. "Yeah, Dad?"

He sighs. "You're going to go through a lot of females. Promise me you won't settle down until you find your mate."

I smirk. "Dad, come on. We don't even know if I have one."

"You do and she's out there," he says, his voice quieting. "Just please, Aric, make me this promise."

I want to laugh off his comment, but I can't. Not with how sad he seems. "Okay, Dad. I promise."

"Thank you," he says.

I kiss Mom on the cheek and jog out the door.

If I knew that this was the last time I'd see my father alive, I would have found something better to say.

Like maybe thank you for being my father.

Dad was always one to sacrifice for the greater good. I'd never learn that this time, the greater good was me.

My friends and I race through the wooded property and toward the rear gate, shoving each other and laughing, betting who will bag the best meal.

Something in the woods lures my attention. I stop as Liam jumps on Koda's back. Koda flips him over and right into Gemini, causing those three to go at it. I edge away from the fight and further away from the path. I'm not certain where I'm going until I find the tree where my father carved his initials and my mother's into a heart.

The scent of scraped wood trickles into my nose. It doesn't make sense, seeing how worn the marks my Dad made are, until I round the other side of the trunk and see a new set of initials placed inside a freshly carved heart.

A.C. that's me, Aric Connor. But who is C.W.?

"Aric, you coming?" Liam asks.

"Yeah," I say, staring back at the tree. "I'm coming. ."

Epilogue

Ten years later…

I steal a glance at the famous Lake Tahoe. The other night, Liam dared me to jump in. At twenty-six, I should be long past taking a dare, except that I'm not. I stripped out of my clothes and dove in. It's already April, but winter is still taking one hell of a bite. Snow still lingers in piles along the sand. I tried not to yelp at the first rush of cold, but then I didn't have to try so hard.

The magic of Tahoe has been spoken of for centuries. Those who experienced it, are awed by its magnificence and purity, the way they speak of it rivalling the way they speak of finding their mates. I've rolled my eyes regarding both several times, dismissing them as gross exaggerations. But since first arriving in the fall and finally experiencing Tahoe for myself, I'm kicking myself for not believing. This place is magic and pure and breathtaking—everything everyone said it was and more. If I had any lingering doubts, they were kicked to the curb the night of my swim.

Each stroke I took further in seemed to draw the Lake's magic deeper into my muscles, vanquishing the ache and sting from the cold as easily as a warm soak in the tub. I decided to take my students down here today as a lesson. These young *weres* don't embrace the responsibilities we have to our world. They're lazy, assuming they can take on any evil that strikes by merely relying on the strengths of their beasts.

On principle, I woke them at four in the morning and worked on their tracking and agility until they collapsed moaning at my feet. They thought I was done. Nothing like running a few hours on the beach to cool them down.

I won't make them run around the entire perimeter. Not this time. But I will if their attitudes don't improve.

The soles of my sneakers dig into the sand as I round the bend, barely leaving an indentation and making even less of a sound. It's hard to maintain my hard-ass persona when the gentle waves splash against the cold moist sand like a lullaby. But I do it. Like I said, these young wolves have a lesson to learn and . . .

The scent of water misting over rose petals fills my nose, sending goose bumps clawing up my arms. I frown, narrowing my eyes at the female who approaches. Like me, she's in running shorts, giving me a view of her thin, muscular legs, while a tight T-shirt hugs her round breasts and flat stomach. She's running at the same pace I am with very little effort and barely a whisper of sound. Her long, thick hair bounces behind her, the strengthening breeze keeping the long strands back and exposing her beautiful features.

Her large green eyes meet mine without hesitation, shimmering in the sun like precious stones dipped in water. My wolf perks up, clawing my insides and demanding out. What's his problem? Spiritual being or not, he's not the one in charge.

This female, woman, whatever she is, is challenging my beast. That's what I think . . . until she smiles, and the world stops and . . . *what the hell is happening*? I furrow my brows, demanding to know what she's up to and damned if I'll be the one to break eye contact first.

We stare at each other, drawing closer, my breath increasing and my insides twisting hard enough to send my heart pounding like a sledgehammer against my sternum.

I grind to a halt, turning as she passes and well aware that I'm no longer frowning. No, I'm very much enticed.

My wolves stop on either side of me, watching me watch her. "Did I tell you to stop running?" I snarl.

I shouldn't yell or growl. Not now. Not when all that exists is her.

I'm barely aware of my wolves resuming their pace as I stand there, my full focus on her as she jogs away. She glances over her shoulder as she continues to run, the wind sweeping her long mane of curls behind her.

I'm rooted where I stand, unable to move, barely able to do more than gaze at her. I tilt my head, certain that I must know her from somewhere. But someone like her would be impossible to forget.

My wolf lurches us forward, insisting we chase her down. I just barely hold him back. I start to turn as she disappears, trying to convince myself that nothing had changed even though *everything* had . . .

Read on as the Weird Girls saga continues with ***Sealed with a Curse,*** the first full length novel in The Weird Girls Urban Fantasy Romance series by Cecy Robson. The excerpt has been set for this edition only and may not reflect the final content of the final novel.

Sealed with a Curse

A Weird Girls Novel

By

CECY ROBSON

<h1>Chapter One</h1>

Sacramento, California

The courthouse doors crashed open as I led my three sisters into the large foyer. I didn't mean to push so hard, but hell, I was mad and worried about being eaten. The cool spring breeze slapped at my back as I stepped inside, yet it did little to cool my temper or my nerves.

My nose scented the vampires before my eyes caught them emerging from the shadows. There were six of them, wearing dark suits, Ray-Bans, and obnoxious little grins. Two bolted the doors tight behind us, while the others frisked us for weapons.

I can't believe we we're in vampire court. So much for avoiding the perilous world of the supernatural.

Emme trembled beside me. She had every right to be scared. We were strong, but our combined abilities couldn't trump a roomful of bloodsucking beasts. "Celia," she whispered, her voice shaking. "Maybe we shouldn't have come."

Like we had a choice. "Just stay close to me, Emme." My muscles tensed as the vampire's hands swept the length of my body and through my long curls. I didn't like him touching me, and neither did my inner tigress. My fingers itched with the need to protrude my claws.

When he finally released me, I stepped closer to Emme while I scanned the foyer for a possible escape route. Next to me, the vampire searching Taran got a little daring with his pat-down.

But he was messing with the wrong sister.

"If you touch my ass one more time, fang boy, I swear to God I'll light you on fire." The vampire quickly removed his hands when a spark of blue flame ignited from Taran's fingertips.

Shayna, conversely, flashed a lively smile when the vampire searching her found her toothpicks. Her grin widened when he returned her seemingly harmless little sticks, unaware of how deadly they were in her hands. "Thanks, dude." She shoved the box back into the pocket of her slacks.

"They're clear." The guard grinned at Emme and licked his lips. "This way." He motioned her to follow. Emme cowered. Taran showed no fear and plowed ahead. She tossed her dark, wavy hair and strutted into the courtroom like the diva she was, wearing a tiny white mini dress that contrasted with her deep olive skin. I didn't fail to notice the guards' gazes glued to Taran's shapely figure. Nor did I miss when their incisors lengthened, ready to bite.

I urged Emme and Shayna forward. "Go. I'll watch your backs." I whipped around to snarl at the guards. The vampires' smiles faltered when they saw *my* fangs protrude. Like most beings, they probably didn't know what I was, but they seemed to recognize that I was potentially lethal, despite my petite frame.

I followed my sisters into the large courtroom. The place reminded me of a picture I'd seen of the Salem witch trials. Rows of dark wood pews lined the center aisle, and wide rustic planks comprised the floor. Unlike the photo I recalled, every window was boarded shut, and paintings of vampires hung on every inch of available wall space. One particular image epitomized the vampire stereotype perfectly. It showed a male vampire entwined with two naked women on a bed of roses and jewels. The women appeared completely enamored of the vampire, even while blood dripped from their necks.

The vampire spectators scrutinized us as we approached along the center aisle. Many had accessorized their expensive attire with diamond jewelry and watches that probably cost more than my car. Their glares told me they didn't appreciate my cotton T-shirt, peasant skirt, and flip-flops. I was twenty-five years old; it's not like I didn't know how to dress. But, hell, other fabrics and shoes were way more expensive to replace when I *changed* into my other form.

I spotted our accuser as we stalked our way to the front of the assembly. Even in a courtroom crammed with young and sexy vampires, Misha Aleksandr stood out. His tall, muscular frame filled his fitted suit, and his long blond hair brushed against his shoulders. Death, it seemed, looked damn good. Yet it wasn't his height or his wealth or even his striking features that captivated me. He possessed a fierce presence that commanded the room. Misha Aleksandr was a force to be reckoned with, but, strangely enough, so was I.

Misha had "requested" our presence in Sacramento after charging us with the murder of one of his family members. We had two choices: appear in court or be hunted for the rest of our lives. The whole situation sucked. We'd stayed hidden from the supernatural world for so long. Now not only had we been forced into the limelight, but we also faced the possibility of dying some twisted, Rob Zombie–inspired death.

Of course, God forbid that would make Taran shut her trap. She leaned in close to me. "Celia, how about I gather some magic-borne sunlight and fry these assholes?" she whispered in Spanish.

A few of the vampires behind us muttered and hissed, causing uproar among the rest. If they didn't like us before, they sure as hell hated us then.

Shayna laughed nervously, but maintained her perky demeanor. "I think some of them understand the lingo, dude."

I recognized Taran's desire to burn the vamps to blood and ash, but I didn't agree with it. Conjuring such power would leave her drained and vulnerable, easy prey for the master vampires, who would be immune to her sunlight. Besides, we were already in trouble with one master for killing his keep. We didn't need to be hunted by the entire leeching species.

The procession halted in a strangely wide-open area before a raised dais. There were no chairs or tables, nothing we could use as weapons against the judges or the angry mob amassed behind us.

My eyes focused on one of the boarded windows. The light honey-colored wood frame didn't match the darker boards. I guessed the last defendant had tried to escape. Judging from the claw marks running from beneath the frame to where I stood, he, she, or *it* hadn't made it.

I looked up from the deeply scratched floor to find Misha's intense gaze on me. We locked eyes, predator to predator, neither of us the type to back down. *You're trying to intimidate the wrong gal, pretty boy. I don't scare easily.*

Shayna slapped her hand over her face and shook her head, her long black ponytail waving behind her. "For Pete's sake, Celia, can't you be a little friendlier?" She flashed Misha a grin that made her blue eyes sparkle. "How's it going, dude?"

Shayna said "dude" a lot, ever since dating some idiot claiming to be a professional surfer. The term fit her sunny personality and eventually grew on us.

Misha didn't appear taken by her charm. He eyed her as if she'd asked him to make her a garlic pizza in the shape of a cross. I laughed; I couldn't help it. *Leave it to Shayna to try to befriend the guy who'll probably suck us dry by sundown.*

At the sound of my chuckle, Misha regarded me slowly. His head tilted slightly as his full lips curved into a sensual smile. I would have preferred a vicious stare—I knew how to deal with those. For a moment, I thought he'd somehow made my clothes disappear and I was standing there like the bleeding hoochies in that awful painting.

The judges' sudden arrival gave me an excuse to glance away. There were four, each wearing a formal robe of red velvet with an elaborate powdered wig. They were probably several centuries old, but like all vampires, they didn't appear a day over thirty. Their splendor easily surpassed the beauty of any mere mortal. I guessed the whole "sucky, sucky, me love you all night" lifestyle paid off for them.

The judges regally assumed their places on the raised dais. Behind them hung a giant plasma screen, which appeared out of place in this century-old building. Did they plan to watch a movie while they decided how best to disembowel us?

A female judge motioned Misha forward with a Queen Elizabeth hand wave. A long, thick scar angled from the corner of her left jaw across her throat. Someone had tried to behead her. To scar a vampire like that, the culprit had likely used a gold blade reinforced with lethal magic. Apparently, even that blade hadn't been enough. I gathered she commanded the fang-fest Parliament, since her marble nameplate read, CHIEF JUSTICE ANTOINETTE MALIKA. Judge Malika didn't strike me as the warm and cuddly sort. Her lips were pursed into a tight line and her elongating fangs locked over her lower lip. I only hoped she'd snacked before her arrival.

At a nod from Judge Malika, Misha began. "Members of the High Court, I thank you for your audience." A Russian accent underscored his deep voice. "I hereby charge Celia, Taran, Shayna, and Emme Wird with the murder of my family member, David Geller."

"Wird? More like *Weird*," a vamp in the audience mumbled. The smaller vamp next to him adjusted his bow tie nervously when I snarled.

Oh, yeah, like we've never heard that before, jerk.

The sole male judge slapped a heavy leather-bound book on the long table and whipped out a feather quill. "Celia Wird. State your position."

Position?

I exchanged glances with my sisters; they didn't seem to know what Captain Pointy Teeth meant either. Taran shrugged. "Who gives a shit? Just say something."

I waved a hand. "Um. Registered nurse?"

Judging by his "please don't make me eat you before the proceedings" scowl, and the snickering behind us, I hadn't provided him with the appropriate response.

He enunciated every word carefully and slowly so as to not further confuse my obviously feeble and inferior mind. "Position in the supernatural world."

"We've tried to avoid your world." I gave Taran the evil eye. "For the most part. But if you must know, I'm a tigress."

"Weretigress," he said as he wrote.

"I'm not a *were*," I interjected defensively.

He huffed. "Can you *change* into a tigress or not?"

"Well, yes. But that doesn't make me a *were*."

The vamps behind us buzzed with feverish whispers while the judges' eyes narrowed suspiciously. Not knowing what we were made them nervous. A nervous vamp was a dangerous vamp. And the room was bursting with them.

"What I mean is, unlike a *were*, I can *change* parts of my body without turning into my beast completely." And unlike anything else on earth, I could also *shift*—disappear under and across solid ground and resurface unscathed. But they didn't need to know that little tidbit. Nor did they need to know I couldn't heal my injuries. If it weren't for Emme's unique ability to heal herself and others, my sisters and I would have died long ago.

"Fascinating," he said in a way that clearly meant I wasn't. The feather quill didn't come with an eraser. And the judge obviously didn't appreciate my making him mess up his book. He dipped his pen into his little inkwell and scribbled out what he'd just written before addressing Taran. "Taran Wird, position?"

"I can release magic into the forms of fire and lightning—"

"Very well, witch." The vamp scrawled.

"I'm not a witch, asshole."

The judge threw his plume on the table, agitated. Judge Malika fixed her frown on Taran. "What did you say?"

Nobody flashed a vixen grin better than Taran. "I said, 'I'm not a witch. Ass. Hole.'"

Emme whimpered, ready to hurl from the stress. Shayna giggled and threw an arm around Taran. "She's just kidding, dude!"

No. Taran didn't kid. Hell, she didn't even know any knock-knock jokes. She shrugged off Shayna, unwilling to back down. She wouldn't listen to Shayna. But she would listen to me.

"Just answer the question, Taran."

The muscles on Taran's jaw tightened, but she did as I asked. "I make fire, light—"

"Fire-breather." Captain Personality wrote quickly.

"I'm not a—"

He cut her off. "Shayna Wird?"

"Well, dude, I throw knives—"

"Knife thrower," he said, ready to get this little meet-and-greet over and done with.

Shayna did throw knives. That was true. She could also transform pieces of wood into razor-sharp weapons and manipulate alloys. All she needed was metal somewhere on her body and a little focus. For her safety, though, "knife thrower" seemed less threatening.

"And you, Emme Wird?"

"Um. Ah. I can move things with my mind—"

"Gypsy," the half-wit interpreted.

I supposed "telekinetic" was too big a word for this idiot. Then again, unlike typical telekinetics, Emme could do more than bend a few forks. I sighed. *Tigress, fire-breather, knife thrower, and Gypsy.* We sounded like the headliners for a freak show. All we needed was a bearded lady. I sighed. *That's what happens when you're the bizarre products of a back-fired curse.*

Misha glanced at us quickly before stepping forward once more. "I will present Mr. Hank Miller and Mr. Timothy Brown as witnesses—" Taran exhaled dramatically and twirled her hair like she was bored. Misha glared at her before finishing. "I do not doubt justice will be served."

Judge Zhahara Nadim, who resembled more of an Egyptian queen than someone who should be stuffed into a powdered wig, surprised me by leering at Misha like she wanted his head for a lawn ornament. I didn't know what he'd done to piss her off; yet knowing we weren't the only ones hated brought me a strange sense of comfort. She narrowed her eyes at Misha, like all predators do before they strike, and called forward someone named "Destiny." I didn't know Destiny, but I knew she was no vampire the moment she strutted onto the dais.

I tried to remain impassive. However, I really wanted to run away screaming. Short of sporting a few tails and some extra digits, Destiny was the freakiest thing I'd ever seen. Not only did she lack the allure all vampires possessed, but her fashion sense bordered on disastrous. She wore black patterned tights, white strappy sandals, and a hideous black-and-white polka-dot turtleneck. I guessed she sought to draw attention from her lime green zebra-print miniskirt. And, my God, her makeup was abominable. Black kohl outlined her bright fuchsia lips, and mint green shadow ringed her eyes.

"This is a perfect example of why I don't wear makeup," I told Taran.

Taran stepped forward with her hands on her hips. "How the

hell is *she* a witness? I didn't see her at the club that night! And Lord knows she would've stuck out."

Emme trembled beside me. "Taran, please don't get us killed!"

I gave my youngest sister's hand a squeeze. "Steady, Emme."

Judge Malika called Misha's two witnesses forward. "Mr. Miller and Mr. Brown, which of you gentlemen would like to go first?"

Both "gentlemen" took one gander at Destiny and scrambled away from her. It was never a good sign when something scared a vampire. Hank, the bigger of the two vamps, shoved Tim forward.

"You may begin," Judge Malika commanded. "Just concentrate on what you saw that night. Destiny?"

The four judges swiftly donned protective ear wear, like construction workers used, just as a guard flipped a switch next to the flat-screen. At first I thought the judges toyed with us. Even with heightened senses, how could they hear the testimony through those ridiculous ear guards? Before I could protest, Destiny enthusiastically approached Tim and grabbed his head. Tim's immediate bloodcurdling screams caused the rest of us to cover our ears. Every hair on my body stood at attention. What freaked me out was that he wasn't the one on trial.

Emme's fair freckled skin blanched so severely, I feared she'd pass out. Shayna stood frozen with her jaw open while Taran and I exchanged "oh, shit" glances. I was about to start the "let's get the hell out of here" ball rolling when images from Tim's mind appeared on the screen. I couldn't believe my eyes. Complete with sound effects, we relived the night of David's murder. Misha straightened when he saw David soar out of Taran's window in flames, but otherwise he did not react. Nor did Misha blink when what remained of David burst into ashes on our lawn. Still, I sensed his fury. The image moved to a close-up of Hank's shocked face and finished with the four of us scowling down at the blood and ash.

Destiny abruptly released the sobbing Tim, who collapsed on the floor. Mucus oozed from his nose and mouth. I didn't even know vamps were capable of such body fluids.

At last, Taran finally seemed to understand the deep shittiness of our situation. "Son of a bitch," she whispered.

Hank gawked at Tim before addressing the judges. "If it pleases the court, I swear on my honor I witnessed exactly what Tim Brown did about David Geller's murder. My version would be of no further benefit."

Malika shrugged indifferently. "Very well, you're excused." She turned toward us while Hank hurried back to his seat. "As you just saw, we have ways to expose the truth. Destiny is able to extract memories, but she cannot alter them. Likewise, during Destiny's time with you, you will be unable to change what you saw. You'll only review what has already come to pass."

I frowned. "How do we know you're telling us the truth?"

Malika peered down her nose at me. "What choice do you have? Now, which of you is first?"

acute bloodlust A condition that occurs when a vampire goes too long without consuming blood. Increases the vampire's thirst to lethal levels. It is remedied by feeding the vampire.

Call The ability of one supernatural creature to reach out to another, through either thoughts or sounds. A vampire can pass his or her *call* by transferring a bit of magic into the receiving being's skin.

Change To transform from one being to another, typically from human to beast, and back again.

chronic bloodlust A condition caused by a curse placed on a vampire. It makes the vampire's thirst for blood insatiable and drives the vampire to insanity. The vampire grows in size from gluttony and assumes deformed features. There is no cure.

claim The method by which a werebeast consummates the union with his or her mate.

clan A group of werebeasts led by an Alpha. The types of clans differ depending on species. Werewolf clans are called "packs." Werelions belong to "prides."

Creatura The offspring of a demon lord and a werebeast.

dantem animam A soul giver. A rare being capable of returning a master vampire's soul. A master with a soul is more powerful than any other vampire in existence, as he or she is balancing life and death at once.

dark ones Creatures considered to be pure evil, such as shape-shifters or demons.

demon A creature residing in hell. Only the strongest demons may leave to stalk on earth, but their time is limited; the power of good compels them to return.

demon child The spawn of a demon lord and a mortal female. Demon children are of limited intelligence and rely predominantly on their predatory instincts.

demon lords (*demonkin*) The offspring of a witch mother and a demon. Powerful, cunning, and deadly. Unlike demons, whose time on earth is limited, demon lords may remain on earth indefinitely.

den A school where young werebeasts train and learn to fight in order to help protect the earth from mystical evil.

Elder One of the governors of a werebeast clan. Each clan is led by three Elders: an Alpha, a Beta, and an Omega. The Alpha is the supreme leader. The Beta is the second in command. The Omega settles disputes between them and has the ability to calm by releasing bits of his or her harmonized soul, or through a sense of humor muddled with magic. He possesses rare gifts and is often volatile, selfish, and of questionable loyalty.

force Emme Wird's ability to move objects with her mind.

gold The metallic element; it was cursed long ago and has damaging effects on werebeasts, vampires, and the dark ones. Supernatural creatures cannot hold gold without feeling the poisonous effects of the curse. A bullet dipped in gold will explode a supernatural creature's heart like a bomb. Gold against open skin has a searing effect.

grandmaster The master of a master vampire. Grandmasters are among the earth's most powerful creatures. Grandmasters can recognize whether the human he or she *turned* is a master upon creation. Grandmasters usually kill any master vampires they create to consume their power. Some choose to let the masters live until they become a threat, or until they've gained greater strength and therefore more consumable power.

Hag Hags, like witches, are born with their magic. They have a tendency for mischief and are as infamous for their instability as they are their power.

keep Beings a master vampire controls and is responsible for, such as those he or she has *turned* vampire, or a human he or she regularly feeds from. One master can acquire another's keep by destroying the master the keep belongs to.

Leader A pureblood werebeast in charge of delegating and planning attacks against the evils that threaten the earth.

Lesser witch Title given to a witch of weak power and who has not yet mastered control of her magic. Unlike their Superior counterparts, they aren't given talismans or staffs to amplify their magic because their control over their power is limited.

Lone A werebeast who doesn't belong to a clan, and therefore is not obligated to protect the earth from supernatural evil. Considered of lower class by those with clans.

master vampire A vampire with the ability to *turn* a human vampire. Upon their creation, masters are usually killed by their grandmaster for power. Masters are immune to fire and to sunlight born of magic, and typically carry tremendous power. Only a master or another lethal preternatural can kill a master vampire. If one master kills another, the surviving vampire acquires his or her power, wealth, and keep.

mate The being a werebeast will love and share a soul with for eternity.

Misericordia A plea for mercy in a duel.

moon sickness The werebeast equivalent of bloodlust. Brought on by a curse from a powerful enchantress. Causes excruciating pain. Attacks a werebeast's central nervous system, making the werebeast stronger and violent, and driving the werebeast to kill. No known cure exists.

mortem provocatio A fight to the death.

North American Were Council The governing body of *weres* in North America, led by a president and several council members.

potestatem bonum "The power of good." That which encloses the earth and keeps demons from remaining among the living.

Purebloods (aka *pures*) Werebeasts from generations of *were*-only family members. Considered royalty among werebeasts, they carry the responsibilities of their species. The mating between two purebloods is the only way to guarantee the conception of a *were* child.

rogue witch a witch without a coven. Must be accounted for as rogue witches tend to go one of two ways without a coven: dark or insane.

shape-shifter Evil, immortal creatures who can take any form. They are born witches, then spend years seeking innocents to sacrifice to a dark deity. When the deity deems the offerings sufficient, the witch casts a baneful spell to surrender his or her magic and humanity in exchange for immortality and the power of hell at their fingertips. Shape-shifters can command any form and are the deadliest and strongest of all mystical creatures.

Shift Celia's ability to break down her body into minute particles. Her gift allows her to travel beneath and across soil, concrete, and rock. Celia can also *shift* a limited number of beings. Disadvantages include not being able to breathe or see until she surfaces.

Skinwalkers Creatures spoken of in whispers and believed to be *weres* damned to hell for turning on their kind. A humanoid combination of animal and man that reeks of death, a *skinwalker* can manipulate the elements and subterranean arachnids. Considered impossible to kill.

solis natus magicae The proper term for sunlight born of magic, created by a wielder of spells. Considered "pure" light. Capable of destroying non-master vampires and demons. In large quantities may also kill shape-shifters. Renders the wielder helpless once fired.

Superior Witch A witch of tremendous power and magic who assumes a leadership role among the coven. Wears a talisman around her neck or carries staff with a precious stone at its center to help amplify her magic.

Surface Celia's ability to reemerge from a shift.

susceptor animae A being capable of taking one's soul, such as a vampire.

Trudhilde Radinka (aka *Destiny*) A female born once every century from the union of two witches who possesses rare talents and the aptitude to predict the future. Considered among the elite of the mystical world.

turn To transform a human into a werebeast or vampire. Werebeasts *turn* by piercing the heart of a human with their fangs and transferring a part of their essence. Vampires pierce through the skull and into the brain to transfer a taste of their magic. Werebeasts risk their lives during the *turning* process, as they are gifting a part of their souls. Should the transfer fail, both the werebeast and human die. Vampires risk nothing since they're not losing their souls, but rather taking another's and releasing it from the human's body.

vampire A being who consumes the blood of mortals to survive. Beautiful and alluring, vampires will never appear to age past thirty years. Vampires are immune to sunlight unless it is created by magic. They are also immune to objects of faith such as crucifixes. Vampires may be killed by the destruction of their hearts, decapitation, or fire. Master vampires or vampires several centuries old must have both their hearts and heads removed or their bodies completely destroyed.

vampire clans Families of vampires led by master vampires. Masters can control, communicate, and punish their keep through mental telepathy.

velum A veil conjured by magic.

virtutem lucis "The power of light." The goodness found within each mortal. That which combats the darkness.

Warrior A werebeast possessing profound skill or fighting ability. Only the elite among *weres* are granted the title of Warrior. Warriors are duty-bound to protect their Leaders and their Leaders' mates at all costs.

werebeast A supernatural predator with the ability to *change* from human to beast. Werebeasts are considered the Guardians of the Earth against mystical evil. Werebeasts will achieve their first *change* within six months to a year following birth. The younger they are when they first *change*, the more powerful they will be. Werebeasts also possess the ability to heal their wounds. They can live until the first full moon following their one hundredth birthday. Werebeasts may be killed by destruction of their hearts, decapitation, or if their bodies are completely destroyed. The only time a *were* can partially *change* is when he or she attempts to *turn* a human. A *turned* human will achieve his or her first *change* by the next full moon.

witch A being born with the power to wield magic. They worship the earth and nature. Pure witches will not take part in blood sacrifices. They cultivate the land to grow plants for their potions and use staffs and talismans to amplify their magic. To cross a witch is to feel the collective wrath of her coven.

witch fire Orange flames encased by magic, used to assassinate an enemy. Witch fire explodes like multiple grenades when the intended victim nears the spell. Flames will continue to burn until the target has been eliminated.

zombie Typically human bodies raised from the dead by a necromancer witch. It's illegal to raise or keep a zombie and is among the deadliest sins in the supernatural world. Their diet consists of other dead things such as roadkill and decaying animals

Photo by Kate Gledhill of Kate Gledhill Photography

Cecy Robson (also writing as Rosalina San Tiago for the app Hooked) is an author of contemporary romance, young adult adventure, and award-winning urban fantasy. A double RITA® 2016 finalist for Once Pure and Once Kissed, and a published author of more than twenty novels, you can typically find Cecy on her laptop writing her stories or stumbling blindly in search of caffeine.

www.cecyrobson.com

Facebook.com/Cecy.Robson.Author

instagram.com/cecyrobsonauthor

twitter.com/cecyrobson

www.goodreads.com/goodreadscomCecyRobsonAuthor

For exclusive information and more, join my Newsletter!

http://eepurl.com/4ASmj

www.ingramcontent.com/pod-product-compliance
Lightning Source LLC
Chambersburg PA
CBHW030026200726
48283CB00012B/1031